In loving memory of my father, James E. St. Sure, United States Marine Corps.

Dad, you fought the great battle. Thank you for leaving me your journals.

M. L. St. Sure

CHRISTINA'S WAR

AUSTIN MACAULEY PUBLISHERS™

LONDON • CAMBRIDGE • NEW YORK • SHARJAH

Ordering Information
Quantity sales: Special discounts are available on quantity purchases by corporations, associations, and others. For details, contact the publisher at the address below.

Publisher's Cataloging-in-Publication data
Sure, M. L. St.
Christina's War

ISBN 9798889105299 (Paperback)
ISBN 9798889105305 (Hardback)
ISBN 9798889105312 (ePub e-book)

Library of Congress Control Number: 2023920277

www.austinmacauley.com/us

First Published 2024
Austin Macauley Publishers LLC
40 Wall Street, 33rd Floor, Suite 3302
New York, NY 10005
USA

mail-usa@austinmacauley.com
+1 (646) 5125767

Prologue

In 1914, two pistol shots signaled the beginning of the Great War, and Joseph Cross, a tall, broad-shouldered twenty-five-year-old opera prodigy, left Austria to become a soldier. He was armed only with his life and sheet music, which he kept in a rolled oat box, and a talisman of golden amber his father had found on a snow-capped mountain when he was a young boy.

With his wife, family, and friends weeping, he sauntered across the stage of the Vienna State Opera, wrapped his blue chinchilla cape over his tuxedo sack-coat, and walked out the door into the blowing snow to join the long row of soldiers marching toward France. He rubbed the rock of amber in his pocket between his fingers, and his panic began to subside.

He thought about his life and the lives of his comrades who marched beside him in great lines stretching across the countryside and about the countless generations that would be affected by the destiny that lay before them. He promised himself that if he ever got out of this war alive, he would never again become so caught up in the business of singing that he would neglect what was going on in his country. He would lay bare what was right and what was wrong.

Chapter 1

Christina Cross dropped to her knees in the plowed furrow. Her calloused fingers tore at a brown line of weeds matted in the hard earth, and then the sun flashed on a crude prism of amber. She looked toward heaven and pledged to change her Austrian stubbornness and sharp tongue as if this was the good luck she always dreamed of.

When the rock finally broke free, she swore her oath out loud this time as she polished the thing in circles with her seed sack. She held it to the sun and peered through the clear amber at the strange creature trapped inside. It had long, threadlike antennae near the center of its head and a tube-like funnel extending downward from its mouth. The body, covered in yellowish armor, had four silver-netted wings and pincer-like growths along its segmented tail.

Two of the three pairs of jointed legs had sharp talons protruding from them. It was frozen in battle, she thought, a creature from thousands of years ago.

Joseph, her father, reined the plow horse toward her, and all the while she thought how out of place he seemed on the worthless expanse of dust he called his farm. His determination to till the unimaginable infuriated her. He had holes in the knees of his ragged overalls, and his face was

M. L. St. Sure is a writer and poet whose work has appeared in several publications. She attended The Iowa Writer's Workshop and soon after wrote her debut novel. She lives in Wisconsin.

gray with dust. He still wore those horrible boots from the Great War.

She glared at the porch clinging to the old shanty, an afterthought slapped together with barn wood siding to make room for more beds. It was only a matter of time before the grove of prickly ash reclaimed the ugly little house. She was certain her father would never consider any sign or omen that would make his life better.

Joseph drew near and caught a glimpse of the golden amber she had tossed back into the weeds. He jumped from the gangplow, picked it up, and cradled it in both hands. His thick, dusty brows drew together and he wheezed out, "What have you here?"

Christina shook her thick black hair from her handkerchief, the only French characteristic inherited from her mother she was truly fond of, and mopped her brow.

She mumbled what her father had said so many times before, "It's probably bad luck."

"Quite the contrary," he said, to her surprise. "When I was nineteen, about your age, my father found a great rock of amber and gave it to me. He found it on a rescue mission, searching for a ski patrol buried in an avalanche. He said it would always bring luck because the men were found alive. I carried it everywhere I went. It was my talisman. And now to think you have come upon the same luck! Something so wondrous has to be blessed."

He held it to the sun and studied the captive insect's dark, bulging eyes. "Fearless, his talons ready for battle— survival, that's what it's all about." He smiled for the first time in years. "It's an omen I have prayed for. Your grandfather believed it to be good luck, and now we have it back once again!"

"Well, we'll need a whole seed sack of luck living here in Kelly Flat," Christina said, giving voice to that old nagging feeling that nothing would ever change.

The image of the beautiful Austrian village in the Krems Valley and all of its flowers and green lawns never left her. The opera her father performed for the élite of society, her mother dressed in French couture sitting on the balcony— all cruelly ripped away by the Great War.

She was only five years old at the time but would never forget the charred hole that remained in her home. She watched her father rub the wound on his neck, the ugly scar a reminder of his greatest loss. She prayed a thousand times he'd recover his singing voice but no matter how hard he tried, the shrapnel lodged between his vocal cords afforded him only breathy, hoarse tones.

Joseph shook the rock before her and Christina let go of her thoughts. She watched the way his blue eyes sparkled. Never in all of her life had she seen him so excited, and she threw her arms around him and hugged him tight. Then and there, the way he cried, laughed, and squeezed her back, she knew they had something together.

The two of them finally became comrades.

"The war and Missouri are bad luck, aren't they, father?"

"At least we have food on the table. I know you think it's a bad life, but it will get better, now that we have our luck piece."

Christina saw the faraway look in his eyes, the expression she went to bed with on many nights. She would wonder what he had been through during the war, wishing for, wanting his conversation, his answers, until finally, she would fall asleep.

"I traveled with your grandmother and grandfather to Sarajevo. I was to sing an opera for Archduke Ferdinand and his wife, but I didn't get the chance," her father was saying.

Christina took a deep breath, afraid to exhale, for fear he wouldn't finish his sentence. "There was an assassination attempt on the Archduke, and we ended up at the hospital to see if we could help the injured. We saw the Archduke's car coming down a side street. The driver was trying another route to get them safely out of town."

"We watched in horror as the assassin jumped onto the running board of the Archduke's touring car and fired a pistol. Two shots: one struck him, and the other his wife. I wasn't twenty feet away, and I chased after him. Without so much thought, I threw the amber rock as hard as I could and hit the young rebel in the back of the head. I'll never forget the look in his eyes as the people dragged him away. The Archduke and his wife died soon after, which led to the war."

Christina thought about the ancestral journals she found in an old trunk in the attic. She marveled at the life her father led in the old country. Surely, it was grand to be an opera singer and grand to fight for the victory of his homeland. He had accomplished so much in his life.

"Please tell me about the war, father. All of my life you have put me off."

"Because it was a terrible thing. A knife in my heart that I'll not put in yours."

Christina was all too familiar with his reaction, the look on his face. Nothing changed in all of those years when the conversation of war was brought up. She watched him turn and climb back onto the gangplow and slap the reins on the horse's rump. Dust swallowed him as he headed toward the barn.

Chapter 2

A storm blew across the prairie, coursing over the old shanty. Curtains fluttered at the broken window and sent a vase of pokeweed crashing to the floor. Christina woke, her heart pounding in cadence with her nightmare. She eyed the shards of glass, then rolled from her cot and carefully cleaned up the mess.

Soon, the red-hot sun rose. She quickly dressed in the yellow hopsack skirt and cotton blouse she had selected the night before, then stepped toward her reflection in the window. She unbraided her hair and brushed the strands, then plaited one long braid again. She walked carefully over the old loosened floorboards and into the kitchen to join her young sister, Nicolette, and her brother, Marcel. A blond curl sprang from Nicolette's thick short hair as she sidled next to Christina, clicked her heels together, and squared her shoulders.

"You didn't practice your singing lesson yesterday," Marguerite, her mother, said as she inspected the crudely mended seams on Christina's blouse. "Your father is not pleased with the *bel canto*, and you'll fall like wheat before a scythe, if it is not precise."

"You've told me over and over again you want to be an opera singer like your father, but you can be certain it will never happen if you don't apply yourself."

"Yes, ma'am." Christina smiled thinly.

Marcel butted in, his Austrian blue eyes glaring for a fight. "She doesn't give a hog's whisker if she gets a licking for not practicing. She ain't even sorry for not helping me and Nicolette with Bible study!"

"Has God answered your prayers?" Christina asked. "He probably never will because He can't understand that twang of yours."

"You ain't ever gonna be saved!" Marcel plopped his hands on his bony hips and tapped the floor with his foot.

"I suppose you didn't tell mother about Sunday mass— tossing that apple core back and forth to Tommy McMurphy behind Father Finnegan's back. Making fun of him, mocking his old age. Poor Father barely noticed when it smacked him in the head!"

"Enough!" Marguerite shook her finger severely. "I won't tolerate such wild stories! Christina, you'll wrap the cornbread for our trip into town. Marcel, you'll gather the berry baskets and load them into the wagon. The lamps need filling, so put the kerosene cans for refilling in as well."

Christina turned on her heels and stomped to the front porch.

Joseph Cross was harnessing the mare to the buckboard wagon; he eyed Christina as she clattered down the porch stairs with Nicolette in tow.

"I want you to be extra good today," he said to her. "Don't spoil your mother's birthday. It's not every day she can do what her heart favors." He turned and watched

Marcel saunter down the stairs and glare at Christina. "Over here, young man," he ordered, then spat on his palms and smoothed Marcel's cowlick. Taking notice of the self-important look Marcel gave Christina, he yanked his son's ear. "Now, pick up those baskets and kerosene cans and load them onto the wagon."

Their mother frittered at the screen door, pulled her muslin shawl snugly around her shoulders, and fussed with her prematurely gray hair.

"Marguerite, we're ready." Joseph smiled.

They traveled the old road that wound through Kelly Flat, a small, quiet town set between forested hills and low plains. Prairie chickens followed the clattering wagon, pecking the ground where crumbs fell from the cornbread. A sleek black Stutz Bearcat convertible purred past, scattering the chickens in all directions, then disappeared around a corner into a cloud of dust.

They stared at the custom-built automobile, and Christina and Nicolette admired the woman sitting inside, dressed in white linen and a harlequin hat. Christina could see the El Dorado Inn on the hill ahead, and as they passed, she glanced along the coneflower-lined footpath leading to a green-and-white striped awning over the entrance. Men dressed in creased pants and starched shirts drank tall glasses of beer on the veranda.

Fickbohm's General Store stood across the street. Old man Fickbohm leaned against the open door, rubbing his round belly and hollering out greetings. He reached into his apron pocket and tossed a rock of brown sugar into Nicolette's lap as they passed by and she squealed with delight. Joseph doffed his hat and smiled.

Christina stepped into the front seat and slid next to her father. "May I please take the reins?" She knew his answer but never gave up hope.

"Yes, you need to get to know this old mare," he said, to her surprise. "The feel, the timing of her—she's as bullheaded as you, but well-tempered to those who know how to handle her." And with that, he placed the reins into Christina's hands.

"Yes, sir!" she said, then turned and smiled purposely at Marcel while he shifted uncomfortably in his seat. She slapped the reins, and Dandelion trotted as fast as her old legs could go.

The Missouri River curled along its channel, leaving swampy backwater and curtains of mist settling along its shores.

"Whoa! Whoa! Dandelion, take her easy." Christina leaned back and pulled firmly on the reins and swelled with confidence as she had pleased her father.

They piled out of the wagon with their baskets and climbed up onto the bluff and into a field of prairie clover. Joseph untied his bandanna and swatted a tree stump before sitting on it. He rolled up his sleeves and breathed deeply, his expression remote. Christina sat quietly at his feet.

He was fair-haired, tall, and hard-set in his ways. Lines etched his face, and hollowness replaced the spark that lightened his blue eyes in years past. He most certainly hadn't envisioned the kind of life he had now. His determination surely outweighed his common sense, Christina considered, but then she knew he was out of his element; an Austrian surrounded by a swarm of mixed nationalities and ideas.

She yearned to know him; his childhood, the war, but he always kept that window to his thoughts curtained and carefully drawn. She wasn't a child any longer. It was time for her to be let into her father's heart. "I want to know about the war," Christina blurted in one last despairing effort. "And please don't tell me I'm too young to know of such things. I'm a grown woman!"

Joseph sat and chewed on a straw as if contemplating a memory, recollecting everything. He watched Marguerite and Nicolette fill their baskets with berries that grew large and ripe among the dead wood. Marcel was shoving berries into his mouth as fast as he could pick them.

"Please," Christina huffed in exasperation. "Your nightmares have kept me awake long enough!"

He shook his head helplessly, surprised at her revelation. The memory of war had not dimmed for him; if anything, it had magnified. He spoke hesitantly, feeling that old uneasiness. "My sweet Christina, since the day I was born, I've known nothing but war and its horrors. It's difficult to talk about, and something I don't want to burden my children with."

"I've got a right to know!"

Joseph listened intently. After much deliberation, he said, "People were more interested in independence than strengthening their monarchy. Soon, the radical nationalists took the matter into their own hands. I was twenty-six when Archduke Ferdinand was shot and killed and war for me became a reality."

"What did you do?" Christina asked.

"I left Austria and joined the Resistance in France and fought a terrible war. I was in the hospital when I learned of

America. An American infantryman, who became my comrade on the battlefield, ended up lying in a cot beside me. He spoke of freedom and how a man could homestead a farm no one could take away."

"It seemed a safe country, a good place to raise a family, and where a hard honest day of work would pay off. He said he would sponsor me and my family. I had no future, no voice, and no homeland. I jumped at the chance to go to America, to Missouri."

He put his head in his hands and stared at the river, lost in thought.

Christina wondered about his comrades and if any were left. It must have been agonizing; the memories, the mingling of cold, hard steel and flesh. Somehow, he seemed to live with it. She watched him lie back on the grassy bluff and stare at the sky. The war was why he couldn't open up, she thought, why he always cut her off. He closed his eyes, shutting her out again.

Carefully, she lifted a hand from beneath his head and gently pressed it to her cheek. It felt hard and rough. As long as she could remember, he worked the land. It was like their life, she thought, dead and disappointing.

She always wanted their life back in Austria; something more: days filled with excitement, something to wake up to besides monotony and drudgery, but father said life wasn't supposed to be exciting, that people expected too much from it. Again, she wondered what went on in his mind— and in her mother's. After living in Austria, Christina knew America was not in her heart and never would be.

She studied the dirt beneath her broken nails and the calluses on her palms and wondered how a father could see people's characters in their hands. Her hands looked like rawhide. What kind of a man would marry a girl with a working man's hands? She would remain a spinster for the rest of her life.

Joseph praised her solid stock, predicting she would blossom into a true beauty due to her good bone structure and strong, healthy teeth. Never did she chew prickly bark to soothe a toothache. She was blessed with her mother's eyes: coal black and flecked with gold. They were Christina's greatest assets, and she could accomplish anything with a bat of her thick, bristly lashes.

Joseph said they reflected independence of spirit, a rare quality for a girl. He commended her for being strong in mind and voice and prodded her to put forth earnest effort in her voice lessons so that one day she would become an opera singer.

He was convinced she would be much better than he had ever been.

Christina watched her mother drink from the jug of water she filled at the pump that morning. She was looking at a prairie chicken scratching for a morsel in the dirt by an old log. Her skin was that of a hired hand, not of a French aristocrat. She was thin and appeared to be tired of life. In reality, Christina thought, living with a man like her father took considerable strength. She wondered what her mother saw in this Godforsaken country.

From sunup to sundown, she worked in the cotton fields, breaking her back from the constant bending and picking of fluffy white bolls alongside Joseph. If Grandfather Pétain knew his precious French doll was picking cotton, he'd rake his son-in-law over the coals. It was no wonder her parents argued bitterly day and night.

Christina's stomach turned at the thought. She watched Marcel loosen a boulder with both feet and send it flying down into the river. He perched on a stump and scanned the bluff for another. He was tall and lanky, and his thick blond hair poked out of his straw hat like pasture thistles. He worked the fields resentfully, constantly complaining and sniveling until father would smack him a couple of times to give him something else to think about.

Marcel always found solace in his mother's quarrel with his father over his punishment. It furthered his aims, wanting to be in his mother's good favor. She obliged his each and every fancy, and it puzzled Christina that father would permit his son to be pampered. Marcel was lazy, pure, and simple, she thought. He would never amount to a hill of beans.

Thunder rumbled from far off, and lightning speared the horizon. Joseph's eyes flicked open and saw Christina's expression as the anvil top of a giant thunderhead crept toward them. "Find your brother and sister, Christina," he said calmly, then stood and brushed his overalls. "Mother and I will hitch the horse and bring the wagon around. Meet us at the bottom of the bluff."

Christina ran down the winding path toward the river and found Marcel and Nicolette wading in the backwaters. "We've got to go!" she waved.

Marcel turned and mimicked her, then dove back under the water.

"I mean it!" she shouted angrily. The sky was an ugly green. Thunder rumbled again, and Nicolette began to cry.

"It's all right," Christina hollered. "Climb up the bank. I'll come for you as soon as I find Marcel." She ran to the river's edge and stepped into the churning water. She heard a clap of thunder again.

"Marcel!" Christina called. She lost her footing on the slimy rocks and felt the bottom drop from under her. The current took her beneath the surface and swirled her end over end. She clawed at the water, kicking out with her legs, the whole of her body thrashing with terror. Her lungs pumped for air, craving it.

She thought of Marcel and the way he looked at her before he dove under the water. She was not going to die like this, not because of Marcel. Don't give up! Fight! Hang on! Her mind beckoned. She struggled violently toward the shore, then grabbed a tree limb and hung on with all of her might.

Her body dragged against the current and broke the surface. She felt the water swirl smoothly past and the rain beat down. Her vision cleared and focused on Nicolette's frightened blue eyes looking down at her.

Little by little, Christina pulled herself up and onto the river's edge. She lay back in exhaustion, coughing up a mouthful of dirty water, and soon it hit. No feeling Christina had ever felt was as fierce as this. One horrible thought after another played out in her mind as she considered a way to punish Marcel, some awful affliction to torment him.

Her face was hot now, her thoughts lost in rage. She rose to her feet and grabbed Nicolette. Their clothes clung to their shivering bodies and their shoes squished water and mud as they ran up toward the wagon. They pulled themselves over the side and onto the seat.

"Bet you thought I was a goner, huh?" Marcel shouted, and his expression twisted into a smirk. "Should've seen your face!"

Christina lunged and clutched his neck. "You beast! How could you?" she screamed.

Joseph cracked the whip. The horse jolted and threw Marcel to the floorboard. Christina fell on top of him and threw her fist into his face. He bawled, and Marguerite shoved Christina aside and pulled him next to her. Joseph laid the whip on Dandelion and she lurched, straining her pull against the sucking mud.

The wagon wobbled and thrashed from side to side in the flooded ruts until the mare came to a halt. Her stiff ears swiveled as she sniffed the wind for what seemed an eternity, and then she reared on her hind legs. Joseph's broad shoulders arched, and his face looked as though his thoughts were filled with terror. He laid the whip across her hindquarters again until her hooves hit back on the ground and she buckled in exhaustion.

"It's no use!" he shouted above the thunder.

Christina dropped from the wagon and sloshed toward the mare, then took hold of the bit, tugging and coaxing until she pulled the mare clear of the ruts. She stroked her muzzle. "Good girl, good girl. You can do it, Dandelion!"

Christina ran to the other side of the wagon and slapped the mare's flank as hard as she could. Dandelion bolted, taking the wagon and passengers into the forest. The wind shrieked through the tall trees, and suddenly a shaft of lightning cracked an old cottonwood tree.

On its way down, it took Joseph with it.

Chapter 3

On a jade green bluff under the shade of prickly ash, a Catholic priest mused on private memories and extended compassion to the small gathering. Christina lifted her gaze to the blanket of wildflowers strewn over the pine box. A horrible ache settled. Never would she see father again. God had snatched his life from her. With an enraged impulse, she shouted, "Damn you, Lord! Why'd you take him? You should've taken me!" She collapsed, sobbing over the coffin.

Several people in the small gathering gasped, and Nicolette ran away crying.

Marcel ran after her and brought her back, kicking and squirming.

"It's going to be all right!" he hollered to his mother.

Christina lifted her head in dismay. "Father's dead! It'll never be all right. God Almighty struck him down and he laid there in the mud." Tears gushed from her eyes and down her cheeks.

Marcel walked to the casket and shook her hatefully. "Simmer down," he muttered. "Mother's got enough worries without you shooting off your big mouth!"

Marguerite rounded the casket with a look that made her shudder. Her voice was low and seething. "You killed him, not Almighty God. If it weren't for you, he'd still be alive. You beat that horse right into the thick of the forest, you witless fool! Why, on God's earth, couldn't I have raised you to be like your brother?" Her eyes found Marcel.

"I was trying to help! I—" Christina watched her mother clutch Marcel's hand and knew right then and there all had been lost.

"Leave!" Marguerite demanded. "You have no place at this gathering."

The words slashed Christina, and she wanted to shout her pent-up anger and void herself of all the injustices but her mother quickly turned and walked away hand in hand with Marcel and Nicolette, and no more was said.

Christina ran back home, collapsed onto her cot, and crawled under the blanket, wishing the world would end. She lay awake that night tossing and turning, reliving the last several days. She could see that her mother's accusation would never pass from her head. They never did when it came to father; it was as if mother was jealous of the attention Joseph gave her, scarce as it was.

She wondered if he was aware of what happened, and what he might be thinking and if he knew it was an accident. Her eyes went to the tattered window screen and watched as it flapped in the hot breeze. She felt her father cloaked in the night wind, and his love was with her. He had promised that nothing would ever come between them. That he would always protect her from lightning storms and all of those black goblins that jumped out from the shadows.

She realized she depended on him forever; his strength, fortitude, and his insight into the workings of the land. She couldn't still believe that he left her alone in the world. How could all of this be possible? She felt breathless, stunned, and she buried her face into her pillow and wept.

"I miss him, too." Nicolette rolled over and stroked Christina's hair. "Remember when father said all we ever needed was a bit of luck to make it through something bad?"

Christina sat up and wiped her cheeks with her palms, struggling with words.

"Only one thing you can count on and it's not luck, Nicolette. It's yourself, nothing more, and the sooner you learn that, the better off you'll be."

She took Nicolette's hand and walked her out to the porch and sat on father's old ladder-back rocker. The wind gave way to the stillness of the rural countryside. An occasional cricket chirp brought a measure of tranquility. Together, they searched the sky beyond the stars into the midnight blue of the universe and watched a brilliant light burst forth and vanish as suddenly as it had appeared.

Nicolette reveled at what she saw and quickly took her father's luck piece from her pajama pocket and toyed with it before Christina. The sight of it pricked Christina. *Father must have given it to her*, she thought. The ache in her heart would never go away. She still felt the spirited words she often mumbled beneath her breath regarding the hopes and dreams the luck piece might grant father. She had pitied him. And nothing had changed.

She looked through the window at the scarlet ribbons tacked on the wall. For her sixteenth birthday, father had given her the *Légion d'Honneur* medallion, which was awarded for bravery, and the distinguished merit medal he had received during the war.

She saw him as a hero for the first time, full of confidence and strength. He shared his poetry and history of Germany and France, the operas of Austria; songs he encouraged her to sing so that someday she might prepare for the Vienna opera as he had. Why hadn't she practiced her voice lessons? Why had she taken his advice and efforts so lightly?

Her thoughts were strangled with questions, more questions than she had answers for. In exhaustion, her head fell upon Nicolette's shoulder and soon they were both asleep.

Chapter 4

Christina emptied her dresser and placed her clothing into an empty flour sack.

She took a deep breath and turned. Nicolette's expression mirrored hers; she knew her thoughts. They stood looking at each other not knowing what to say, simply foreseeing the inevitable: waking without one another, playing, working, surviving, and everything else without the other. Nicolette broke the silence, scooped up her kewpie doll, and placed it into Christina's flour sack.

"Father won it for you at the state fair," Christina protested. "He wanted you to keep it."

"But she'll remind you of me."

"How could I ever forget you, my little sweet pea? I love you more than anything in this world. I'm only leaving for a short while, long enough to set us straight again."

"You promise you'll be back soon?"

"Sure as biscuit root blooms in spring."

Christina smiled reassuringly and studied Nicolette's little waif's face and crooked little grin. The thought of leaving broke her heart. She followed Nicolette's gaze out of the window. The clouds muted into dull gray, and Nicolette focused on Dandelion chomping the carrot tops and potato skins that Marguerite had given her. "Marcel said he is the boss of the family, now that father's gone," she sniffed. "Why can't *he* go instead?"

Christina turned Nicolette to face her. "Marcel will never take father's place. Never!" she said firmly. "And I will see to it that you live in a grand house someday. I'll buy you a closet full of dresses just like Grandfather Pétain bought for grandmother, and perhaps an ounce of Evening in Paris, a radio, and a new doll."

"Desperate people do desperate things," Marcel said as he sauntered into the bedroom. He leaned against the wall and ran his fingers through his matted hair, then squatted before Nicolette. "Don't you go gettin' any ideas? Your big sister's got them pipe dreams, and you know them never come true."

"Not so!" Christina inspected Marcel's look of superiority. "You'll never take father's place. You'll never walk in his shoes!" She grabbed the flour sack and began filling it again, ignoring Marcel's backtalk.

"Sweet pea, would you please go downstairs and bring me another sack?"

Christina watched Nicolette run down the creaky stairs. She snatched Marcel's ear and tugged him up at eye level. "You'd better take good care of Nicolette while I'm gone. I'm counting on you. Mother won't be any help."

"I'm telling!" Marcel yelled.

"I know what you're up to, you and mother both. I saw you drinking in the barn." Christina felt resentment surge as she always did when her mother drank, and lately, there had been twice as many mason jars scattered about in the old barn.

"Well, who wouldn't, with the likes of you around? That berry wine is the only thing that keeps ma sane!"

"Someone needs to earn some money!" Christina stifled the urge to whack him upside the head, as her father had done. "I can't count on mother! Are you going to help or stand there and flap your jaws with that horrible twang of yours? You do that on purpose just to get under my skin. You are Austrian through and through!"

"It's you!" Marcel poked his bony finger at her chest. "It's you that makes everything wrong. Just like ma says, you're high-spirited, never satisfied, always wanting something better, never accepting of how God flung you on this earth. We'll get along without you. Go! Get outta here!"

Christina grabbed his finger and twisted it until he hollered. "There'll come a day when you'll thank me, thank me plenty because it'll be me and only me who'll fill your belly!"

Christina finished packing and then worked on chores in the barn that were neglected since Joseph died. The hot afternoon wore on. Christina lifted her eyes from the grindstone and sniffed something cooking in the house, and her stomach rumbled with hunger. She thought of the feasts of long past: marshmallows toasting on corncob fires, wagon rides on cool summer evenings.

Those days were growing dim, her vision blotted by worry and hard work. She continued sharpening the cradle scythe, then pumped well water into a dishpan and washed her face and hands. She scurried to the small kitchen overlooking the blackberry patch. Marguerite was scooping bubble and squeak from a cast-iron skillet into earthenware bowls. The oven door was open; sweet potato pie was ready to be eaten, and coffee brewed on the back burner.

Christina entered the kitchen, and the aroma of cabbage, chicken, and brown biscuits made her stomach rumble again. Not since Joseph passed had Marguerite been sober enough to cook, and the sight overwhelmed Christina. She peered around, remembering the kitchen vibrant with her father's songs; a room to live and laugh in and enjoy what food they had together.

The walls were faded, streaked yellow by the sun, but father had ordered a gallon of paint from old man Fickbohm and mother had selected a bolt of cretonne. Christina guessed the curtains wouldn't be hung nor the walls painted, as mother lost interest in just about everything of late. Marguerite poured a cup of coffee, then drew a stool to the hearth and sat down. Her face wrinkled with a miserable frown when Christina entered the kitchen.

Christina smiled. "It's good to see you feeling better."

"Your brother tells me you think we can't manage while you are away."

Marguerite said flatly.

Christina wondered what else Marcel had discussed with her. "Yes, ma'am," she replied.

"Why is that so?"

"I'm worried about the work that needs to be done."

"No need. Marcel will see to it that everything is taken care of."

Christina sat, trying to master her anger. "He won't! You know darn well he won't!"

Marguerite stood. Her face was controlled. "And you would be a fine judge!"

"Mother, he has to take on more responsibilities. I won't be around to do his share."

"He is perfectly capable, always has been. You have made up your mind to leave, so be it. We will get by without you."

Christina dropped her head in her folded hands, and her thoughts went sadly to the chill in her mother's voice. It was always there; her resentful expression and undertone. She lifted her head and stared her mother in the eye. "I best be on my way; I have a long walk to the El Dorado Inn before sunset."

Christina knew that further conversation would lead to stormy waters, and nothing but trouble would come of it.

Mother's silence pulsed with resentment, which had worsened of late. She credited it to father's death, something that would never be forgotten or forgiven. God help those who help themselves, she thought as she looked out of the window at Marcel sitting under a cottonwood tree.

He was of no use to anyone. He had neither the shrewdness nor the will to survive. He would die sitting on his lazy haunches, unwilling to reckon with the crust of the hard-baked earth, and again she wondered why their father hadn't raised him to be a strong, honorable man like himself.

There was no need to delay her departure. Marguerite had already left the kitchen and was headed for the barn. Saying goodbye to Nicolette would be just about the hardest thing she'd ever have to do. She quickly dressed in a cotton print dress, then walked to the outhouse and sat on the plank.

The structure creaked and groaned and the wind blew dust through the half-moon, and chickens pecked at the ground below. Her disgust was tempered with the thought of indoor plumbing; porcelain bowls and sinks with cool water piped into faucets. There were probably hundreds of conveniences she had never seen at the El Dorado Inn. For the first time, she realized how little she knew of the modern world.

She closed the door, hooked the latch, then walked up the stairs and peeked into the bedroom, hoping Nicolette would be napping. Nicolette smiled sweetly in her sleep, and Christina smoothed her platinum curls from her face and kissed her.

"I love you," she whispered. "You'll be in my prayers, and when I return, we'll count the stars in the Heavens, and perhaps we'll find father in one of them." She pressed the amber luck piece into Nicolette's hand, quietly backed out the door, picked up her belongings, and left.

It was evening before Christina approached the green-manicured gardens surrounding the El Dorado Inn. It was a palace compared to the shanty she had left behind. Matronly women in plumed hats and silk dresses sipped tea and gossiped on the veranda. They turned and stared as she walked past and entered the kitchen. A short, round man jumping with quick steps threw an apron in her path. He had small eyes and an impatient, complaining face. Sweat poured from under his chef's hat.

"Put this on!" he puffed. "Make it snappy!"

Christina caught the flying apron.

"I don't have all day, my dear. Put it on!"

Christina frantically wrapped the white starched cloth twice around her waist, then picked up her sack and scurried into the kitchen.

"Over here!" He waved. "Clear this mess!"

Christina dropped her sack, picked up the stack of dirty bowls from the counter, and whirled toward the sink. Her elbow grazed a tray of crystal goblets and sent it crashing to the floor.

"Clumsy oaf! Who were your references?" he asked indignantly.

Christina dropped to her knees and began picking up the shards of glass, not believing what happened.

"Me," a tall, fleshy, red-haired man said as he lumbered into the kitchen. "Do you disapprove?"

The chef met the cool appraisal of Bert Meyer, the hotel manager. He stiffened.

"Sir, it was nothing. No problem at all." He shooed Christina aside and dashed for the broom closet.

Mr. Meyer smiled apologetically and escorted Christina across the room. "Please sit down, Miss Cross." He slid a chair beneath her. "You'll find the chef a bit temperamental on occasion."

"I'm terribly sorry!"

He filled a crystal glass with water and placed it before her. "Please," he said with a smile.

Christina nodded in gratitude and drank the cool liquid. He watched as she savored the drink. Her ebony hair hung in long, loose curves framing her tanned face, and there was a soft color on her full lips. Her dark, sad eyes lit a flicker of entrancement.

"Mr. Fickbohm said you live in Kelly Flat, quite a long way from here," Mr. Meyer said.

"About ten miles."

Mr. Meyer shook his head knowingly. He was well aware of Kelly Flat. Gandy dancers poured in by the thousands to build the railroads. When their work was finished, they left and farmers moved into their abandoned shacks. The land was useless. Broke their backs for nothing. Empty pockets and desperate dreams. Nobody could survive that hellhole of a place, he thought and continued to stare at her.

"Forgive me, but I can't believe you live in such a—"

Christina lifted her eyes and sighed, feeling that old shudder of humiliation.

"Such an awful place? That's why I'm here. I need this job. I'm used to hard work; I'll do anything."

She glanced around the room at the mural-painted walls, the polished floors, comfortable chairs, and rosewood sofas, the fixtures of polished brass and silver candlesticks. It was beautiful, she marveled. Nothing like she had ever seen.

She remembered her father describing this place, the old southern mansion purchased and restored by Senator Liam Caradine. A retreat for the wealthy. Rooms had been added around the old courtyard. Marble floors, crystal chandeliers, and yards of crimson velvet embellished the interior. Each room had its own veranda that overlooked the fountain in the center of the courtyard. In the distance beyond the leaded prism windows, pasture grass rolled like waves on an emerald-green ocean.

"I'll see what I can do to make your stay more comfortable," Mr. Meyer said, gently covering Christina's hand with his own.

Christina scanned his hawk-like eyes and quickly withdrew her hand. "I'd better get to work, sir. I'm sure the chef has plenty for me to do. Please accept my apology. I'll more than make up for it, you'll see."

She stood and walked into the kitchen. The dinner guests were demanding and impatient and treated Christina as if she were worthless. The men weren't as cruel; they thought she was sweet and rather pretty. However, the women rolled their eyes and lowered their voices so she wouldn't hear their petty remarks. They contemplated her hair and tanned face, her calloused hands, and scuffed shoes. The responsibility of seeing they were content and amused was nothing like Christina ever imagined.

At last, dinner was over. She had no idea people took so long to eat. And the wine, my God, how much wine had she poured? She had broken two dishes and one crystal goblet and figured an entire week's wages were now accounted for. She cleared the last of the fine Meissen china from the tables and brought them into the kitchen. She dipped her hands into the soapy water and washed the porcelain. The dishes were perfect white circles with gold monogrammed letters.

When she raised them to the light, she could see her fingers through them. She wondered if the hotel guests were aware of poverty or even thought about it—poverty so mean and hopeless, it was shameful. How easy and soft it was for them, she thought. She knew she was different, would always be different but she would work hard and do well because her pride demanded it.

Christina peered from the window and up a hill. Outlined against the sky, she saw houses, their windows lit with candles. She paused, trying not to worry about Nicolette.

She thought of a new home for her. Homes like those up on the hill with big soft beds and clean sheets and warm blankets and food in the cupboards. She stood thinking and wishing. A lullaby came to her mind and she began to sing. She walked into the dining room, polished the tables, and sang again softly, freely, and alone with her thoughts.

Mr. Meyer leaned casually against the doorway. He watched Christina sweep from table to table. She sang beautifully, he thought. The lullaby was sad, like her eyes; haunting, the color of night reflecting the candlelight as she bent to extinguish the flame.

He caught her glance. "There's a vacancy coming up. A nice room across from the courtyard."

"Why, thank you, sir," Christina said politely, "but I've already made arrangements for a room."

"It'll be convenient."

She eyed his grin and said nothing.

"Well, my dear, if you break any more dishes, you won't be able to afford it." He flicked his cigarette, then threw his head back and laughed.

"It won't happen again, Mr. Meyer, and please take it out of my pay. I'll work overtime to prove myself."

"No matter, I'm sure we can work something out." He rubbed his bushy red beard.

She wanted to tell him she was not persuaded by his sinister thoughts and to go straight to Hades, but the seriousness of her situation outweighed her impulse. It was very apparent that this job was going to entail much more than she'd bargained for, and she'd have to do some serious plotting to outfox Mr. Meyer. She made up her mind that he wasn't going to ruin her only chance for a better life.

The days faded one into the other, and Christina caught herself regarding the hotel's female guests, women who dressed in fine silk and had nothing better to do than chat over tea and had no other thoughts than what to wear the next day. Their bored stares and casual regard for everything but themselves were all she could think about.

The stories she'd heard were true: too much money and idle hands were the devil's playground. They had everything life could offer, yet they complained, sulked, and sniveled for more finery. Even worse, she never escaped Mr. Meyer's scrutiny. He shadowed her night and day, inventing all kinds of excuses to be near her. She saw it all: his gambling, drinking, cursing, and making no effort to mask his sins.

All too soon, he found the vacated shanty she took refuge in and kicked the door open. He reeled from wall to wall and back again in a drunken stupor. Poverty and hunger she could shoulder but what lay ahead would be unbearable. He tore her nightdress from her, and she stood shivering from fright. She had endured his innuendoes, vulgar talk, and stares to keep her job. She lived every night and day, dreading what might happen next.

Now, his huge body fell on top of her and his hands groped her. His eyes were mean like a loathsome reptile's.

She screamed and kicked and scratched, but the more she struggled, the more he enjoyed it.

His red beard was soaked in whiskey. He drooled across her face, and she bit his nose until the skin tore away. She would not let this devil of a man thrust her back into poverty. She was earning a wage and her family was depending on her, but even with this risk, she could not stand this. She would rather die than submit to him. A terrifying thought raced through her, and she wondered if all men were like him.

Christina continued to claw, bite and kick until at long last she was able to knee him in the groin. He rolled from her onto the floor, grabbing himself. He was gasping for air and she wondered if he was dying. He looked like he was slipping away; his body giving up his ghost, and she knew he was going to hell for what he had done, and the fires would burn him to dust.

She gathered herself, then grabbed his ankles and dragged him outside, pushing him down the steps. She watched in relief as he struggled to his knees and crawled away.

Chapter 5

Senator Liam Caradine stared over his bespectacled nose at the skinny girl standing before him. He was an immaculately dressed man with thick white hair framing his lined face and green eyes. His voice was inflected with a slight drawl, just enough to enhance his southern charm.

"When Mr. Meyer first hired you, he suggested I meet you. I apologize for not doing so, seems I've been too busy." He smiled sheepishly.

Christina offered a nod and her heart sank. She would be dispensed an ultimatum; that cruel old devil, Mr. Meyer, was going to see to it. She wanted to blurt out the whole ugly truth but had been told a woman's voice, on such matters, was worth about as much as a Saturday night bath without soap.

"He was reporting to me daily on your progress," Senator Caradine said. "I fired him, you know. Caught him making the rounds with a maid. I'm glad she explained the whole horrid story. Glad he's gone. I heard rumors for some time." He motioned across the room toward the marble hearth. "Please walk for me, Miss Cross."

"I beg your pardon, sir?"

"I'd like you to walk to the hearth and back again."

"But I don't understand—"

"I wish to observe your carriage."

He scanned her appearance as she walked toward the hearth and back again, and then motioned to the chair beside him.

Christina sat looking at her hands. So Mr. Meyer was fired, she thought. She was ecstatic about that. Soon, she became uncomfortable under Senator Caradine's scrutiny and wished he would get on with it—fire her, do something; she hadn't time for this mysterious hogwash.

There was a rap at the door, and a tall, slender man with a gray mustache entered the room.

"I've been expecting you, Murphy." Senator Caradine walked from his desk and greeted him. "I'd like you to meet Miss Cross. Christina, this is Mr. Murphy Carroll, our pianist."

"I'm pleased to meet you," Christina said, bewildered.

"Mr. Meyer heard you singing while you were working in the kitchen. He was quite impressed with your voice and suggested perhaps you might be qualified to sing for our guests in the main dining room."

"What?" Christina gasped.

"I'd like to hear you sing." Senator Caradine motioned Murphy toward the Chickering and placed sheet music from the Wiegenlied Brahms Lullaby on the case. Christina sat completely baffled and could barely compose herself from the shock of it all.

Her eyes flitted to Senator Caradine, and then to Mr. Carroll. She watched his long, slender fingers begin to press the keys, and soon the sweet memories of every song her father taught her flooded through her. Joseph's face seemed to rise out of the music, filling the room, his singing voice in perfect sync; the voice of Baron Ochs in 'Der Rosenkavalier'. She forced herself to stifle her sudden tears, sensing this to be one of the many tests she would face in life. She had to go through with it.

She rose from her chair and trod toward the piano. The words came slowly, softly at first, and then as the tempo swelled, the beauty of the music moved her, swelling and subsiding like controlled breathing in an operetta. It was the fuel that drove her. She was relaxed, her voice strong; she was experiencing the glory her father talked about.

Senator Caradine watched her breathing deep and controlled and the lyric strong and clear. How beautifully she sang, he thought. The room filled with the lullaby, and the words repeated in his mind.

The song coursed exquisitely, and Christina thought of her father; she knew he was within her spirit, the force that spared her and the severing of mind from the unbearable aches and pains of both her heart and body. Then the crescendo; breathing controlled, lyrics from the belly, finale, and suddenly the spell lifted, and she looked about the room as though waking from a dream.

"Miss Cross, you're wonderful!" Senator Caradine rubbed his hands together, and capitalistic inspiration took over. "You'll be perfect for the job! Who taught you?"

"My father." Christina smiled proudly. "But I didn't take opera seriously until he died. He studied as a young man growing up in Austria, and his hard work paid off. He was in demand after his performance in 'Der Rosenkavalier' in Dresden."

"But you sing as if you had composed the score yourself."

"It was one of father's favorites." Christina's elation dissolved into a wistful sigh, and she looked at the piano he had so yearned for. "He would've loved this piano." She couldn't drag her eyes from it. She brushed her palm across the rich mahogany case, then inspected the keyboard and peered inside at the steel strings and hammers.

"He played?"

"Up until the war ended." Her thoughts became hard with memory and she pulled her vision from the piano. "He lost everything; his cello, his harpsichord. When he fled Austria, the only thing he took was his sheet music. He kept it in a rolled oat box in his dresser until the day he died."

Senator Caradine examined the siege in Christina's face. "I'm sorry," he said. "It was a terrible war. We can only pray the world will never witness such death and destruction again."

"I miss him so much." On top of all that, she missed Nicolette desperately. She worried night and day over her welfare, the memory far too fresh of her pitiful existence and Marcel's rankle toward her safekeeping.

"I lost a brother to the war," Senator Caradine said sadly.

"There'll be plenty to do when you return. What with arranging scores and costume fittings and rehearsals, you'll be one busy young lady."

Christina's footsteps faded down the hall, and he peered after her. She felt it, turned, and smiled gratefully.

**

The dust sifted between Christina's toes as she trod the road that stretched before her. Clouds appeared sodden with rain, then went away and reappeared again. Drought left parched vegetation and deep cracks in the earth. Weeds grew green in the gullies and reminded her of the lush, fertile valleys once covering the area. Father had seen it, she reflected, but not nearly enough.

Somehow, he thought he could beat it, fight nature at every turn and suffer the loss. Triumph burned into his mind, and hardship seemed to make him all the more determined. He knew everything except for the cold hard fact the earth couldn't feed his family.

Christina kicked the dirt. "I won't be fooled by you. I won't depend on you for anything!" A puff of dust drifted in the hot breeze and she watched it, her mind whirling with plans. With the money she would make singing for the hotel, she could start saving, move into town and buy a house. It would be a grand place; whitewashed with shuttered windows and a shingled roof. A bedroom each for mother, Nicolette, and Marcel, and a kitchen with enormous windows flooding with sunshine.

Heavy rain clouds gathered again, and she held her head back and tasted the sprinkles. The wind blew, sending tumbleweeds, leaves, and puffs of dust at her. She scurried toward home and soon spied the metal corrugated roof between thatches of mesquite and listened to it pop as it expanded in the heat. She sped down the path, into the yard, and raced into the house.

"Nicolette! Mother! Where are you?" She stepped into the kitchen. Mother was lying on the floor and Nicolette was huddled in a corner.

"Why did you leave me, Christina?" Nicolette blinked away a tear. "Everything's turned bad since you left. Mother's drinking the berry more than ever, and Marcel's been taking it out on the barnyard cats with father's whip. I'm afraid to go in there anymore, even to milk the goats!"

"My poor sweet pea, I should've known!" Christina brushed the splattering of mason jars aside and rolled Marguerite over. She smiled helplessly, exposing her wine-stained teeth. Christina carefully wiped her face and applied a cold towel, thankful that her mother was still alive.

Marcel rushed into the room and plopped on a chair. "Mother doesn't quit drinking till she's out cold," he whined, then removed his undershirt and ripped it into strips, and wrapped his slashed hand. "She was coming after me, outta her head for more wine, but I fixed her, I smashed every jar I could get my hands on!"

"Why didn't you send for me?" Christina shouted. "Why'd you wait so long? I would've come, you know I would've!"

"Just one darn minute; you knew what was goin' on. You can't blame me—you're the one who left!"

"I warned you plenty of times and all you were good for was excuses. You're good for nothing, Marcel!" She looked at Nicolette and her stomach gnawed. "You scared the living daylights out of her. Look at her! Turn and look at her! What do you suppose she was thinking when you were throwing your fit? And what's this about those poor helpless barnyard critters? You've turned into a monster!"

Marcel glared and stomped from the room.

"Oh no, you don't! You march your pitiful backside right back in here and help me. Pick mother up! Then we're going to the barn!"

Marcel turned and shuffled toward his mother.

"Bless my soul, I came home when I did!" Christina pushed him to his knees. "I just pray my plan will work to get everyone out of this stinking hole!"

"Don't matter none to me," Marcel sneered and carried mother into the bedroom. "Pa'd be sick'a hearin' you talk like that. I'll never leave. I was born and raised here. I don't want nothing else, no matter what kinda high-flying job you get!"

"Father would be the first to tell us to get help, you fool! But you don't want help, do you? You don't want to help yourself or anyone else." Christina squatted and pulled the chamber pot from under mother's bed. "Empty this and keep it empty; the flies are thick in here!"

"Ma can empty her own thunder mug."

"Why, you lazy pig! Just as soon as I can get her well, I'm getting her and Nicolette out of here, away from you!"

"Over my dead body!"

"That'll be easy, Marcel. You're already dead!" She grabbed him by the waist and spun him around toward the door.

"Now outside! To the barn!" She shoved him with all of her might out the door and down the winding path that led to the barn. Inside, the mother cat, her litter, and the old tomcat lay scattered. Insects hummed from one bloody heap to the next in a feeding frenzy.

Marcel snickered, looking at them, and Christina hated him—hated him with a force that overwhelmed her. "Thou shalt not kill!" she screamed, watching the lifeless carcasses. "You hypocritical heathen! You learned nothing from the Bible! You beat their hides from them!"

Christina knew, as sure as she stood there, that she could not be born of God, for God would forgive, resist evil, and stand firm. She would tolerate Marcel only long enough to get mother well, then she'd leave him to fend for himself.

She ran from the barn and collapsed against the old water well, looking at the field of half-grown cotton surrounding her. The plow lay in a patch of weeds, abandoned. She stood there shaking with rage, listening to Marcel shriek obscenities. All that was Austrian, all that was father in her, would endure his cruelty. She would leave him in the dust.

**

Christina examined the rows of cotton stalks, standing hardy and mature acre upon acre. Old man Fickbohm and his five sons had taken pity on her and offered their help. She promised to split the profit but he wouldn't hear of it. "Your pa helped me out once, and I owe him big," he said.

Christina threw herself into the task of harvesting the cotton. After the first long day, she fed and watered Dandelion. She was dead tired and could barely get herself from the barn to the house. Mother sat on the porch mopping her face with a rag, and Nicolette stood by her side twirling a ballerina she fashioned from a fuchsia blossom.

Christina hobbled up the stairs. Nicolette skipped into the house and then reappeared waving a letter. "Open it,

Christina," she said excitedly. "Read it to me. A man in one of them fancy automobiles delivered it this morning."

Christina smiled lovingly at Nicolette and sat on the rocker, and pulled her up on her lap. She carefully opened the envelope and slid out a piece of paper embossed with a drawing of the El Dorado Inn.

Her heart sank.

"What is it?" Nicolette asked.

"It's something I carelessly neglected, sweet pea, and I'm ashamed for being so thoughtless." Senator Caradine's last words to her went over and over in her mind: a new beginning, a life singing, a chance to realize her father's dreams.

She had abandoned Senator Caradine without as much as a word, an explanation. The few days she promised him she'd be gone had stretched into the beginning of harvest. Since leaving the El Dorado Inn, she had thought long and hard about another plan to set her free, and about the countless obstacles that could soon grip her dreams and shred the only hope she had left.

Perhaps she had made a mistake. Returning to sing for Senator Caradine would have produced more money than harvesting the cotton. A sudden breeze caught Nicolette's flower ballerina and it drifted into the water trough. Sadly, they watched its delicate pink dirndl fill and settle to the bottom. Christina had to do something, and an apology would be the beginning. She nodded, aching for things gone.

"Why don't you go home for a while?" he said compassionately. "Sometimes we all need to do that." Christina brightened.

Chapter 6

Senator Caradine saw Christina's eyes ringed dark with circles, her blistered skin, and rough hands. He poured tea from a silver service into a china cup and placed it before her. There hadn't been a word in weeks, and her welfare had weighed heavily on him. "I'm so glad to see you!" he said.

Her cup rattled on the saucer, and she placed it back on the curio table. "I'm sorry, sir. Please forgive my thoughtlessness."

"What is it, Christina? What can I do?"

"I want you to know your kindness and generosity have been the nicest thing that has ever happened to me." Her eyes welled and she dared not blink.

"Tell me," he asked. "Is there anything I can do?"

Christina took a deep breath, still struggling with an explanation. She looked away, out of the window, for a long time. Then she looked back at Senator Caradine. "My mother's in a bad way. My father's death was really hard on her. There are times I think she'd like to die and be with him again." The pain began. "Sometimes I feel that way."

"Please, Christina, please don't ever think like that," he lightly scolded. "Life is too precious, too short. I want you here. I want to help you."

"I need to harvest the cotton and sell the crop," Christina replied.

"You can't do it alone!"

She tried to think of an answer to ease his mind. How could she ask a man she barely knew to take on her responsibilities, and why would he want to? She knew the immense differences between them. She laughed inwardly for having dared to imagine she could fit in.

"Why do you care what happens to me?"

"Your voice. It's something so rare. I can't let you throw that away."

Christina felt her face flush and wondered if his preoccupation with her was genuine.

"You have everything to gain, and I have nothing to lose," he spoke impatiently. Christina knew somewhere along the way she had to trust again and build a new life. To realize her dream and, in turn, fulfill her father's dream. Perhaps life would change for the better.

Senator Caradine was convinced her voice was the best of her. Her spirit began to rise. Each day might dawn as an exciting adventure, a day in which she would meet new challenges and new people, she thought. She prayed for the strength to trust.

"Well?" Senator Caradine peered eagerly into her face.

Christina smiled politely. She would have food, money, and clothing, and the knowledge that heartened her most was the thought of singing. Perhaps it would drive out the terrible loss she felt. Perhaps there was a God after all, she thought. Senator Caradine looked at her softly now and there was something in his expression, like her father's when he soothed her aches and pains away, and suddenly she let go. "I won't let you down, sir."

"Forget the harvest, I'll take care of that. Bring your family. I'd like to meet them. I have plenty to do around here; I'm sure we can work something out."

Christina returned home to persuade her mother, Marcel, and Nicolette to begin a new life in town. Marcel dragged an onion crate from under the kitchen shelf and straddled it.

"Beatin' you up'd give me great pleasure right 'bout now. If anyone ever deserved to suffer, it's you after what you did to me." He swatted a fly and began to pull its wings off; first one, then the other and flicked it at Christina.

"Nope, I'll never leave, not the place father broke his back for. Hard work and some prayin' should turn her around. Now get the hell out of here! Go! Run with your tail between your legs to your sweet-smellin' senator! Reckon he's got the patience of a wolf anyways with you flirtin' and battin' your eyes like a toad in a hailstorm at him."

Fury almost choked Christina. She saw the littered house and yard, and buckets filled with garbage and cockroaches. She pointed to a stack of dirty dishes. "Look at this place! You're the one father would curse! You're weak and lazy, and you'd rather die than admit the truth!" He sickened her, and it was all she could do to ignore his amused grin. "And most of all, I'm sick of your twang! Your belligerent twang!"

She thought of father and how the Southerners had taunted him. They called him a rotten German traitor. They were like a burr in his shoe, constantly poking and picking at him. "But most of all, I'm sick of people looking down their noses at us and eating rabbits and squirrels and all the rest of it!"

She kicked a pile of dirty clothes across the floor. "I'm throwing these feed sacks into the compost and lighting a match, and I'm going to send Nicolette to school, and I'm going to hire a nurse to look after mother. You'd best swallow your spiteful pride, brother dear, or you'll rot where you stand!"

Marcel crossed his long arms and laughed. "I'd rather rot!" He flicked his head toward the door. "Now get outta here. I'm gonna make somethin' out of this place, and you'll be darn sorry you ever left. I'll make pa's dreams come true if it's the last thing I do, and someday you'll come crawlin' back!"

Christina shuddered at the thought. It could never be done. Father had already given his life, and nobody had tried more diligently than he. She glared at Marcel. Why did his mockery challenge her so? "You're a darned fool," she said. "Worse than that, you're a blind fool. You'll end up dead, buried alongside father!"

Marcel's gaze swung over her. "And you'll be stretched out in a pauper's grave alone with your high and mighty self 'cause no one else'll have you! You've forgotten who you are—a nothin' from a nothin' town!"

Christina's spine stiffened, her emotions tongue-tied. A thousand horrible names leaped about in her brain but she couldn't think of one foul enough to call him. She peered out of a rusted hole in the screen door beyond weeds that grew high by the porch, at the cemetery on the knoll and father's cross. He had been foolishly stubborn also, she thought. Perhaps it was the penchant, the inclination, which was absolute, in the soul. Marcel would never change, no matter the grief, no matter the battle, for it was just there.

Marcel stood gloating, then shuffled from the room. Christina knew he was laughing and it left her empty.

**

Hotel gardeners wheeled in terracotta pots planted with magnolia trees and placed them around the stage. Christina sat on the floor, her long slender legs crossed under her cotton print dress. She watched an artist put the finishing touches on a backdrop. She saw Nicolette peer around it. "When can me and mother see your dress, Christina?" she asked excitedly. "Can we see it before tomorrow night? Oh, please!"

She held out her pink-dotted Swiss dress and whirled around, then curtsied and blew kisses around the room. Her squealing chatter filled Christina with happiness, and security struck something she hadn't felt in a long time. Fear seemed to have been the only emotion she had memorized.

Tomorrow evening, she'd endure it once again, but there would be no room for failure. She couldn't bear the thought of going back to the old shanty and all of its choking dust and deprivation.

Senator Caradine slipped into the room and watched as Nicolette continued to prance. He walked behind Christina. "I hired the wrong woman," he stooped and whispered into her ear.

She turned and caught his amused expression. "You may be right," she said with a laugh. "Nicolette's certainly more relaxed than I'll ever be."

"Think of your strengths, believe in yourself, and the audience will, too," he said reassuringly. "I know you can do it. The most important ingredient for success is resolve, and you've got plenty of that."

"You really believe in me, don't you?"

"You bet. There's nothing you can't do if you want it bad enough. Sky's the limit." He pulled a chair over and sat down, placed his hands on his knees, and eyed the floor.

He sighed.

"What's wrong?"

His gaze was unblinking, still focused, as if looking away would break his resolve.

"You remind me of someone," he spoke at last. "Someone I loved very much." He looked at Christina and the floor again.

Christina stared at him, feeling embarrassed and flattered at the same time. There was constant adoration fixed in his eyes for weeks, and he had become very protective of her comings and goings. He worked hard night and day to settle her mother and Nicolette in the hotel. He bought furniture and clothing and they ate the finest food.

"Today is my daughter Kara's birthday," he continued. "She would've been about your age by now."

Christina stared aghast, feeling foolish for her silly thoughts. How could it be?

He had never mentioned a daughter before. "The horse threw her, broke her neck—" his voice trailed, and he visibly braced himself. "My wife, Jorgie Vee, couldn't cope. She died a year later."

Christina looked away, feeling sick. She couldn't imagine what he suffered; the loneliness, and most of all, her own presence a constant reminder of his loss. He stood and quickly slid his sleeve over his eyes. "Forgive me. It's been a long day."

"There's nothing to forgive. I'm so sorry for your loss."

He shrugged and smiled self-consciously. "Life has become a pattern of loss until now. Sometimes I wonder how I've lived with it for so long. I hate to admit it, but somehow my life seems balanced now that you're here. A pretty young stranger with a lovely voice and fair skin and a dark crown of shining hair, so much like my daughter. I only wonder what it would feel like to forget. Just once to be carried away from the pain."

Christina sensed something and the struggle began in her mind. Perhaps it was affection misconstrued. Perhaps he indeed loved her as a woman and not as a reminder of his loss. Perhaps it was grief, apprehension, guilt, or a combination of it all that muddled his thinking of her place in his heart. She already knew he would be her path to happiness and if he would permit it, she could love him so easily.

**

Christina listened to the whispers and shuffling of chairs and feet through the stage curtain. She paced back and forth while thinking of losing her voice or forgetting her song chiseled away, and she wished the night was over. She inspected the white satin spilling over her hooped skirt and tugged and adjusted, only to snag it with her rough hands.

Despite her comeliness, she felt like a fraud, a fraud dressed in fancy dreams. Painted lips, eyes, nails, lashes, brows, perfumed oils, powders, and rouge, all the trappings of the rich, yet the hands of a farmer. Perhaps Marcel's opinions were justified, she loathed to admit. At least, he knew where he fit and was honest and faced it squarely.

Her doubts suddenly vanished as she watched her mother walk through the stage entrance. She was beautiful, like she had never seen her before. Her gray hair was gathered in a knot at the back of her head and tied with a black silk ribbon. The emerald green of her dress brought out the steel gray, almost blue of her eyes, and her thin freckled face was rouged and powdered. Christina unpinned her rose corsage, walked toward her mother, and fastened it on her shoulder.

"Where's Marcel?" Mother's eyes darted around the room. Christina tensed, smelling the aroma of blackberry on her breath. "I said, where's Marcel? He was supposed to meet me here!"

"He was?" Christina was shocked that he had left the farm.

"He's taking me home," Marguerite said matter-of-factly.

"But I thought you liked it here! The beautiful room Senator Caradine arranged for you, and our plans, I was going to buy us a house and—" Christina's thoughts tumbled, rendering her speechless.

"Don't pressure me! I don't belong. I don't fit. Anybody with half a brain can see that!"

It was more, Christina thought. She didn't want to fit in or belong to anyone. She was untouchable, stone cold. Her soul belonged in a bottle and Marcel was coming to seal it.

"I won't let you go. You'll die back there!"

Marguerite fixed a smile on her face and nodded.

"What about Nicolette? How can you do this to her? How can you be so selfish?"

Marguerite ripped the corsage from her dress and threw it to the floor, then reeled toward the exit.

Christina frantically searched for words to bring her back but they lay on her tongue like pitch to a tree. She heard the conductor tap his baton. "Mother, will you wait?" She pleaded. "Will you listen to my song?"

Christina scurried to find her position. The stage curtain slid open, and a stream of light momentarily blinded her. She searched the dark shapes stirring in their seats, hoping against hope her mother would be there. She looked quickly toward Senator Caradine and he nodded. This was it, time to begin, and she dared herself not to think about her mother. She eyed the conductor and he tapped his baton twice this time.

The soft sounds of the violins began to fill the room. She took a deep breath and once again struggled to forget the tumult. *Forte-piano*. The conductor swished his baton. Song, the remedy, she ran repeatedly in her mind. The remedy for her soul, words written by those who lived and breathed it. It would deliver her, become her shield, a safeguard perfectly tuned and vocalized to accomplish her ends.

Father, give me strength, she prayed. She eyed the audience, wondering what it would take to please. She felt good to be there for them, a release, comfort to lose herself in song, her certainty seemed to show in their faces and she brightened. Her voice flowed with vibrato; words, dear words of her father's song.

The conductor smiled, pleased with her preeminence, and the audience nodded in approval, swept up in the beauty of her voice. At last, she had released the poverty; the days soaked with exhaustion, the nail-biting ache of it all. She was sure she had captured their hearts. The audience rose and shouted accolades. She curtsied time and time again, breathless from happiness.

The stage curtain swept by and she followed it smiling and waving until she saw her mother and panic came back. Marcel held Nicolette tightly and scurried Marguerite toward the door. He looked back at Christina and shook his fist. His voice was raw and cruel. "If you ever try to take Nicolette, I'll have ma call the sheriff!"

The curtain swept back again, and the lights illuminated Nicolette's blonde curls bouncing as she struggled to set herself free. Christina ran with her arms outstretched, sickened at what Marcel was about to do. "No! No! No!" she cried. "Mother! You wouldn't do that, would you?"

Marguerite squeezed her eyes as if to shut out a bad dream and then her expression twisted with revulsion. "You destroyed the only good thing in my life," she shrieked in French, "and I'll not have you destroy another!" The exit door slammed and Christina slumped against it.

"My God, what's wrong?" Senator Caradine shouted. "What's going on?" He jumped from his seat and ran onto the stage toward Christina. He gathered her into his arms and watched her eyes flutter shut.

**

Fire spewed from shoaled crevices. Embers ignited the darkness and descended through black clouds of smoke. A jagged split opened beneath Christina's feet and she fell into a molten mass, spiraling into an abyss. The world became an inferno of flame. An explosion burst upon her ears as the trembling earth blew in twisting convulsions, one jolt after the other.

It was the damnation of hell, she believed, and then there was silence, and she heard a voice whisper her name. Through the haze she made out a face, her image reflected in those green eyes, and she felt as if she were floating on a cool soft cloud. Her eyes cracked open, and Senator Caradine smoothed her hair and eased into a smile.

"Don't worry," he comforted. "The doctor gave you a sedative. You were in pretty bad shape."

Christina wanted to speak but her tongue felt heavy and the room was spinning.

Her mind rushed, thoughts darting here and there.

"Please, just rest," he said and placed his palm on her forehead, then nudged her back onto the pillow. Tears welled and Christina wanted to bury her head in father's lap and have him kiss her tears and speak soothingly to her. If only he were here. "Oh, father, father!" She thought of the security she felt as a child; how he read her thoughts and calmed her fears.

Senator Caradine sat down beside her and spoke comfortingly but somehow the words seemed hollow, and he struggled with the realization. "Your mother is sick, Christina," he said. "No one can help her, not you, not anyone. She laid her suffocating nature on Marcel, and he is a victim of her sickness. He is probably at war with himself; self-esteem battling weakness, unable to understand either himself or anyone else. Your relationship with your mother reminds me of the ducks in the pond near the river."

"I've watched them on my walks lately, and I've noticed that sometimes a female with ducklings meets another and her young will shift to the other duckling. Seems it's her quacking that attracts them. The more she communicates and swims with them, the more youngsters she lures. Some double their flock while others swim off in isolation. Do you understand what I'm trying to say, Christina?"

"But what of Nicolette? She's the one who will suffer. I can't bear to think of what will happen to her. I'm the one who has taken care of her, not Marcel. All he did was neglect her and it'll happen again as sure as sin on earth!"

Christina knew Marcel's actions would haunt her forever and no one would be able to pound them from her memory. She must think of something to get Nicolette back; and Marcel, mother, no one would stand in her way once she had done so.

She wanted to stop thinking of it; the running of her mind over and over of the responsibility her father had placed upon her when he died. She wished she could run away somewhere; she didn't know where she didn't care; a magical place where she could go to sleep and wake with the realization that it was all just a bad dream.

Senator Caradine fumbled in his pocket for a handkerchief and dabbed her eyes.

"I'll do everything in my power to make sure Nicolette isn't in harm's way. I don't want you to worry because in time everything will work out, you'll see. You have to have faith and trust in me. Meanwhile, I have some good news."

He smiled, desperately trying to distract her. "After the doctor left and you were resting comfortably, I went to my office. There was a message from my good friend, Major Nicholas Miller. He enjoyed your performance, and he'd like you to travel to New York and sing for a special envoy arriving from Europe in a few weeks. It would be a wonderful opportunity for you."

Christina blew her nose. If only she could close her eyes and not see Nicolette struggling to free herself from Marcel.

Senator Caradine looked out the window at some faraway place, then back at her. "I don't think you know what you've brought to my life," he said, realizing for the first time that if she accepted the offer to go to New York, he would be without her for a while.

"You've given me feelings I thought were long since dead. You made me feel joy and real happiness, and I've struggled with my conscience time and time again trying to put everything in perspective—whether you were my long-lost daughter or a full-grown woman who only needed a kind heart and a strong hand to hold." He lowered his eyes.

"Please don't think of me as an old fool."

Christina laced his fingers with her own and pulled him to her bosom. She was filled with sorrow and tried to sort things out. Senator Caradine's intelligence and driving ambition had captivated her.

Unselfishly he introduced her to a life she only dreamed of and it was only on this night, this miserable night when the ache of it all was so unbearable, she realized how desperately she needed him. With him, she would be absent from the Godforsaken fear. He would get Nicolette back and protect and take care of her. A thread of strength came into her and she ran her fingers gently through his silver hair. Never had she known such sweetness.

Chapter 7

Laurent de Gauvion Saint-Cyr leaned forward in his leather armchair, patted his pocket for a cigarette, and then remembered he had given them up. His hard angular face concealed his anxiety. He had been taught and disciplined in all the strategies of war and came to know what lay behind mortal calculations.

"I have been invited by the American Major Nicholas Miller to observe West Point. He wishes a reciprocal observation." His voice was level and firm and his keen blue eyes saw relief in his chef d'état-major's face; Jean-Baptiste Mercier was a taciturn, tough-jawed former prizefighter.

"I shall accompany you, sir," Jean-Baptiste said enthusiastically.

Laurent stood behind his desk and approached Jean-Baptiste. "You are aware, for France's sake, we need a collaborator," he said, "and a powerful one; this is an opportunity of a lifetime."

The plan took shape gradually in his mind, a plan shouldered by desperation. He thought of justice, there was none, only the hand of fate. It was fate the rearmament of Germany by an astute young lecturer had taken place. Laurent eyed the bronze statue of France and skimmed its inscription: *Liberté, Égalité, Fraternité*, then inspected the oil painting above it of his great-grandfather.

His blue uniform was simple, bereft of the plume of Rhine Army generals. A modest, powerful, and precise man, marshal and peer of France, state minister in counsel with his majesty, and Grand Cross holder and member of the *Légion d'Honneur*, the son of an artisan from Toul who had reached the first rank of his profession alone and seemingly without effort.

"Quite a man, sir," Jean-Baptiste said in admiration.

"Tell that to Napoleon," Laurent said sarcastically, unnerved at the bitter contempt he still held. He thought of the two men: Napoleon, impatient and greedy, his orders executed without consideration for difficulties or human forces.

The general, on the other hand, had one set of values, rules of reason. He discussed arrangements that seemed ineffective to him, measured the obstacles, calculated the risks, and did not seek to force events. "Grandfather was infallible in the eyes of his men. It explains his career under Napoleon."

Laurent knew he was greatly changed by what his grandfather lived through. Changed for the better, otherwise he could not contemplate the horror that lay before him.

"His refusal of the appellation by Napoleon," Jean-Baptiste assumed and then said it out loud.

"Renouncing the title of duke was the smallest price he paid. The Russia expedition—wise men led to slaughter by a fool. Only Napoleon could've concocted such a plan. Grandfather insisted he abort. It was a political and military error from the beginning but Napoleon wouldn't listen. The bastard! And now this man Hitler, a modern embodiment, reinterpreting the same scheme."

He felt alien, as alien and forsaken as if he had come from another world. Something had gone from the French. What was it? Had they become desensitized? Immune to the brutal circumstances? Their problems had been his problems, their needs his needs, but they had reacted differently than he to the threat posed by Hitler. They were losing their world to a madman.

The shrill sound of the bullhorn announced the graduation rehearsal to be held on the main parade ground in front of the Cadet Chapel at noon. Laurent thought of what lay ahead. His head throbbed. He knew what others had only surmised. "Jean-Baptiste, please make the necessary arrangements. It will be an honor to observe Major Miller's technical virtuosity. Also, relay my utmost gratitude."

"Yes, sir." Jean-Baptiste saluted, pivoted, and then marched out of the room. Laurent methodically paced the terrazzo-tiled floor. His powerful, well-muscled body moved with restless energy. He gazed out the tower window across the boulevard at the war ruins of a bygone era. Laurent felt hell rise in his thoughts. Napoleon had known about power, and his power had perished by its excess. It always would. No man could master his destiny; that is, no man at war with himself.

From his vantage point high on the officer's platform, Laurent scrutinized each minute detail. The battalion's cadence was flawless. A sea of blue and gold moved with the precision of a single man as the band trumpeted *La Marseillaise*.

The president of France and his cabinet of ministers stood at attention and saluted the passing flag. The *feu de joie* concluded the ceremony. One thousand cadets lined perpendicular with the battalions aimed their rifles and shot after each command across the sprawling gardens into the setting sun. This was graduation for a select few—a select few who would be receiving commissions to serve in France's Regular Army.

The military ball was held in the *Croix de Guerre* Room. Massive casements filled with medals of war dedicated by Louis XIV lined the marble walls, and hand-painted murals depicting Napoleonic Wars sheathed a domed ceiling. Cadets stood *en grande tenue* flanking a single expanse of red carpet.

They eyed the *corps diplomatique* and *grande dames* as they made their entrances through gilded doors and mingled with the French élite. The air soon grew heavy with the scent of perfumed lobes and powdered faces: the smell of the affluent. An open out-of-door concert began playing below the grand balcony.

Hundreds of people gathered to listen and watch colored lights sparkle on the cypress trees below. Laurent watched Duchess Aimée of Montrose from across the room. She was smiling now that she had seen him. He knew she was not through with him yet. He strolled toward her and touched his crystal goblet, brimming with Château Margaux, to hers.

"I've missed you," he said, then drained his glass.

Aimée fingered her emerald necklace self-consciously, then placed her wine back on the serving tray. She followed his blue eyes as they searched the curves beneath her silken gown. "How could one love and hate so consistently?" she asked.

"Pride is indeed the virtue of misfortune."

It had only been a few months, Laurent thought, yet somehow, it seemed an eternity since Duchess Aimée's royal wedding; the day that sealed her loneliness forever. He would never forget it; words had leaped from her lips as she made the ascension toward the altar: "I love you," she whispered desperately, and then the long dead silence as she waited for a sanction, a nod, a word, something from him he could not give.

It seemed she had stood and looked for an eternity with those love-hate eyes he came to know so well. He nodded impatiently toward her groom, and he knew she longed to slap him then and there.

"So, you miss me." Her voice was crisp. "I'm certain your soul exists in that horrible place of darkness between Earth and Hades. You are impulsive," she admonished, batting her blonde lashes. "You've no reason to miss me."

"Your pursuit was his patrician title, was it not?" Laurent asked, catching the eye of the Duke of Montrose from across the room.

"My d'interest affaire is no concern of yours," Aimée replied.

"Oui, but it is."

"So, you care?"

"I always will." He studied her expression, and her color heightened as their eyes met.

The Duke of Montrose glared across the smoke-filled ballroom at Lauren and then snatched another whiskey from the *dame de compagnie*'s silver tray. He tossed it down, sucked in his stomach, smoothed his thin hair, and then as casually as his will could muster, he wove his way through the crowd, nodding at people. "We meet again."

The duke extended his hand. "I hope I haven't intruded," he said sarcastically.

"No such luck, my friend," Laurent replied lightly and gripped his hand. "Just a simple conversation between two old friends."

"Old friends, old lovers. I overlook nothing, as I am also a connoisseur of beauty. She's exquisite, of that we agree. The gold of her hair, skin the color of peaches, and a face and body men would kill for. I've hit it big, and all I can offer you is pity for your misfortune." He smiled smugly, then turned attentively toward his wife and guided her to the dance floor.

As they danced, Aimée watched Laurent, his head held high like that of a prince, the white of his dress jacket contrasting with the tan of his face. He smiled a smile that sent her pulse racing, and she returned the same, knowing she would see him soon.

**

The swift cold wind of the *mistrals* blew over the countryside, leaving icy tentacles in its path, and the full moon sparkled on the rushing waters of the Loire River. The *château* was nestled in a peaceful wooded valley; its stark stone walls were crowned with battlements, scarred by war during the Middle Ages. Aimée restored all authenticity and preserved the fortifications merely for tradition.

The gatehouse, which was the innermost and strongest portion of the *château*, had been completely gutted and redecorated and was now a stately country home. Persian carpets lay on white Italian marble, and furniture from the Napoleonic Era embellished the interior. Works by El Greco, Carracci, Rubens, Velazquez, and Van Dyck lined the walls.

Despite the chill outside, Aimée had lavished in a hot bath and smoothed perfumed oils onto her skin. Now she carefully selected a black silk dressing gown from her armoire. She would always go back to that place in her heart and mind, that place of longing, of lust for things that could never be. He would come to her full of eagerness and frustration tonight but only for a stolen moment and then he would leave again and her heartache would begin anew. Why had God not answered her prayers for a thousand nights?

She peered from the *brise soleil,* then pulled the door open and looked down the footpath across the vineyards. Shadows streamed across the grounds in the moonlight and wind rustled the cypress trees. He was late, much too late. She worried and then cursed at the thought of rejection.

Suddenly, she saw him on the footpath and ran from the *château*. He stumbled toward her and into her arms. She struggled, guiding him inside, and propped him on a *couchette*. "You are late, and worst of all, drunk!" she said wildly. "Did you really think it would take such a mountain of courage to meet with me tonight?"

The lively twinkle in his eyes infuriated her even more. "Nothing's changed! It's still the same!" She cried and slid her thumb across the rouge on his lips. "You *farceur!* You're horrible!"

"You are like dangling bait before me." He forced a laugh. "By the way, where is your duke?"

"It was your decision not to marry me!"

She was right, Laurent thought. Who was he to criticize? He smiled feebly and then shrugged.

Aimée helped him to his feet and maneuvered him up the stairs and into the bedroom. He fell back onto the bed, and she began to undress him. Soon, he lay naked before her. He was tall, raw-boned, with muscled shoulders, and she reveled at the pleasure that was hers for the taking. She quickly disrobed and pressed her body onto his and softly traced his lips with her fingers.

There was a rugged, vital power about his face; it haunted her, always had, and now she thanked God for the comfort of him. It felt good to have him beside her again; to lay close, feel the hardness of his body, and know he stood like a steel barrier between her and loneliness. She was hopelessly in love with him, and it was of no use to resist, far beyond her control. Her lips slid slowly down his body, tasting him, drinking in his male scent.

Tonight, she would memorize his tough, lean physique. Tonight, he would be hers.

The Duke of Montrose lay rigid with fury, glaring at the ceiling. His mind raced, and he shuddered with humiliation at the thought of his wife slipping from his bed. How could she be so brazen? Did she really think he had fallen asleep? Did she think he was so naïve? Naïve enough not to monitor her *affaire d' amour*? It came to him frighteningly that it was all over, and deep inside, he could not accept it.

Suddenly, he felt as lonely as if he were the last being on Earth. He felt outside of something he couldn't control. Something had gone from him, a feeling of power and domination, and in its wake, he had grown far too complacent. Now she was gone and with her, she had stolen his happiness. She had left behind a broken old man who would carry undying bitterness to his grave.

He thought again for a long while about his life and how he struggled with difficult situations; how all of his conviction, power, and authority could not sway fate, and then he slowly began to smile. Broken, yes, he realized, but anything was possible when necessity prodded, and he would hold securely onto the things he knew best. She would soon know his cunning. He would be empowered to make things right. There was a way to rid Laurent of her life once and for all and bring her crawling back.

He laughed. He was glad he helped finance the young orator. The rearmament of Germany would soon be a reality. Glory was ripe for the taking. He thought about his new rank in the SS: Colonel. It pleased him, and he liked the sound of it, Colonel Joachim Montrose. It made him feel young again, virile, masterful, and forceful.

He sat up and lit a cigar. He thought of his mission, part of the vast scheme. The groundwork would soon be complete. It was curious how everything played into his hands. How plans, by the cunning of his exploitations, had been arranged into a single conspiracy. Defiance, revolution, and subversion, all arranged. His work was a brilliant maneuver, a *coup d'éclat.*

Soon, he would take his rightful place among the Germanic order. He poured himself a drink. He had only to wait; it was decreed. Let her have her moment of *grande passion*, he thought with a laugh. He would soon have her all to himself for the rest of his life. He breathed deep, and the rage slowly subsided. It felt like he was coming to life again after being dead. He poured himself another drink.

Soon he would be a man at peace.

Chapter 8

Laurent watched the Hudson River wind through a narrow green valley swept with high, craggy shores. The tall, pointed rocks reminded him of the castles on the banks of the Rhine.

He examined his reflection in the window and then shrugged despondently. His eyes were puffy and red from lack of sleep. Time was passing. He had to return to France, and the sooner the better.

The Communist Party and Fascist groups were growing rampant, and it was only a matter of time before his homeland would be at war. His visit to West Point was well worth the two grueling weeks of observing army weapons, field maneuvers, and endless military parades. Public relations were of utmost importance now, and it was reassuring to know he had gained the favor of Major Nicholas Miller.

He scrutinized a platoon of West Point cadets exercising a precision drill in front of Washington Hall. So many fine, dedicated men, he thought. War would ruin France if she was not prepared, and he had seen firsthand what the Germans had done to Czechoslovakia. He knew what they were capable of.

Major Miller walked into the room and placed his headdress on a settee. He smoothed his silver hair, then fumbled a hand into his coat pocket and removed an envelope.

"It's from Governor Carlstrom. Please accept my apologies for being late. He can talk the holy hell out of a person. You know these politician types."

Laurent smiled. "Yes, Major, there is a French expression, *âmes de boue,* which means 'souls of mud'."

Major Miller laughed. "I guess they're the same the world over."

"May I?" Laurent scrutinized the envelope.

"Please. Governor Carlstrom wouldn't hear of me inviting you informally. He wanted it engraved, and all expenses on the taxpayers."

Laurent slid his finger under the gold seal and removed the invitation to the military ball. He sighed tiredly and dropped it on a pile of letters.

"I know you're anxious to return home," Major Miller said sympathetically. "I've heard the rumors."

"Unfortunately, they aren't rumors. It's a scheme that'll disrupt the world. This man, Hitler," Laurent's voice became thick with anger, "How could anyone not see? How could your country not see?"

"We know little of him. He is indeed an enigma," Major Miller agreed.

"Well, I know him, and I'm telling you, he's determined to win back Germany's glory. He's a skillful schemer and organizer and plans to rebuild Germany into an empire that will last a thousand years. His words hypnotize those who listen, but some of us see past him, and we aren't going to sit and wait for a miracle."

"Is France prepared—militarily?"

"Unfortunately, France is also fooled by him. Many eyes must open before we can prepare, and I intend to devote my last breath to that purpose. I'm not some mad prophet—the world will bear this war, and, somewhere along the line, you and I will face the same battlefield."

"Our world has endured many battles, not one provoked by us," Major Miller said, "but if our security is threatened, I assure you, we'll act with everything we've got to save ourselves. And, yes, somewhere down the line, it may well lead to a battlefield in France, but if it does, you'll face an ally."

An American collaborator. Laurent couldn't ask for more. He thought of France and the barriers that had to be conquered. He would have to unify her people. He could not command where there was an argument. Germany held the sword: order, harmony, men made to conform to the disciplined order of an army, a people dedicated to the cause.

If France refused logic, if she were not prepared by sacrifice, unity, and commitment, she would fall. He thought of his mission. There were many who believed in him: the French *Maquis*, named after the tough, scrubby vegetation on the Mediterranean coast, men synchronized to fit into a scheme of sabotage, a cinder in Germany's eye.

Still, Laurent ached for France. She'd win the lobbed battles by German forces, but she wouldn't win them all. He doubted Major Miller had a clear vision of what was militarily possible—the profound impact Germany would have on the world. He had to provide him with the broadest and clearest picture of Hitler that was possible.

"Perhaps our conversation will be of interest to your governor," Laurent prodded.

"Tomorrow evening, we'll address the matter," Major Miller said. Inwardly, anxiety burned, something he could not appraise. Perhaps it was fear, Major Miller thought.

War in Europe would mean war here. Why hadn't they been thoroughly briefed on this man, Hitler? Why all the obscurity surrounding him? Why America's neutrality? He thought how interesting it was that Americans voluntarily put war out of their minds, including himself. Oh, he knew about Czechoslovakia and the Sudetenland, a border area inhabited by people of German origin since the Great War.

After all, it was their land, and he supposed Germany had a right to it. He hadn't given it much thought, not until Laurent had deemed it a reality. A master race, he had said. A master race has chosen to dominate the world. It had the makings of a nightmare.

Laurent walked up the granite steps to the entrance of Washington Hall. The *médaille militaire* with its yellow and green ribbon and scarlet-ribboned *Légion d'Honneur* shone like precious gems among the war medals lining his white uniform jacket. He glanced down at them with pride; commendations of courage, things accomplished, and chronicles of his life.

Again, he thought of war and what it would do to his homeland. He knew it would change him, not just physically, but mentally. Events propelled rapidly during the war, each hour an eruption of motion, weariness, and anxiety so intense it wrested years from a man's life. He entered the smoke-filled room, surveyed the crowd, and then jostled toward Major Miller.

"I'd like to introduce Governor and Mrs. Carlstrom," the major said, motioning toward a short, stocky man with jowly cheeks who was standing next to a woman with flaming red hair and lips to match. "Governor and Mrs. Carlstrom, this is Laurent de Gauvion Saint-Cyr."

Mrs. Carlstrom's alabaster face creased into a wide, flirtatious smile. "It is my pleasure," she said.

Laurent removed his hat in a bow and kissed her wrist.

"You're everything I've read about and more, if that's possible," she said, panting like a giddy schoolgirl.

Governor Carlstrom shook his hand. "Don't mind Sheila," he apologized. "Shyness has never been her strong suit. Welcome, I hope you've enjoyed your visit. Nothing like New York, eh?" He pulled out a cigar and jiggled it between his fingers.

"She's a grand old city, she is."

"Don't start with New York," Mrs. Carlstrom interrupted. "I'd like to know more about this charming young man." She ran her eyes over his trim physique. "They say you're the catch of the century, and I can certainly see why. Seems I read about an engagement," She rambled, "a countess, princess, or—"

"Have you a light?" Governor Carlstrom asked, frantically pawing his pockets, hoping to change the subject and deliver Laurent from his wife's grip.

Laurent flicked the cover off his lighter and lit the cheroot. The governor inhaled and hacked out a brown cloud. He hacked again; this time, the wrenching spasm doubled him over.

"Honestly!" Mrs. Carlstrom said impatiently. "I've lost my train of thought now."

"Please, please, it is fine." Laurent smiled an embarrassed smile. "Madame Carlstrom, you are right. My *affaires de Coeur* appear to be important matters for your American press, but I can assure you, I have, as you Americans say, many wild oats to sow. My *bonne compagnon* is a matter of the past."

Duchess Aimée's beautiful face was embedded in his thoughts and for a moment he tasted her tears, felt her impotent frustration as she pounded his chest with her tiny fists. Never had he the time or inclination to nurture a relationship. His life was his country, an obsession seated in his genes and handed down from a generation of military predominance.

Mrs. Carlstrom smiled and her small brown eyes gleamed. "Do I have a girl for you? My niece, Sarah, she'd be perfect!"

She caught her husband's frown, then glanced at Laurent and shrugged. The lights grew dim, then bright, signaling the guests to the Roosevelt Room for dinner. Mrs. Carlstrom looped her hand through Laurent's arm and coaxed him into the dining room.

When the guests were seated, Major Miller walked to the speaker's podium.

"Ladies and gentlemen, before we begin our dinner, I'd like to say a few words. I'd like to welcome the many dignitaries who took time from their schedules to join us this evening. Governor and Mrs. Harry Carlstrom, Senator Gerald Kohl, Congressman James Eugene, and New York City Mayor, Mr. Zachary Patrick."

"It is also my pleasure to introduce our special guest this evening. He graciously accepted our invitation to tour the academy and discuss new military techniques in weaponry, field maneuvers, and engineering presently being explored in Europe. He knows well, indeed, what one hundred and forty years of turning out quality officers mean to us."

"The École Spéciale Militaire de Saint-Cyr was established by Napoleon Bonaparte in 1802, the same year Congress established West Point. Napoleon appointed his top general, Laurent de Gauvion Saint-Cyr, to institute an academy for his army. He was the most brilliant of generals in the old Rhine Army."

"His genius conceived bold plans with stamina and wisdom. We have much in common, the general and me. The same philosophy, goals, and desire to turn out the best men possible."

He paused for a few moments, second-guessing the reaction of his next words.

"Soon, France will need these men." He scanned the crowd. Judging from the murmurs and the exchanged looks his words elicited, it was on everyone's mind.

"Yes, there will probably be war. A war bigger than anyone can imagine, and it's time we acknowledge that fact. It's time to look ahead, time to prepare for the inevitability. We must not fool ourselves regarding Germany's intentions. We stand insulated, wrapped in denial, while a palpable force gathers strength and cunning."

"I think of France, a country suffering the expectations of an invasion, being brave, yet dubious of the magnitude of the thrust that will crush her doors. There will come a day when we will inevitably suffer the consequence of our detachment."

"To deny the cause will hurt us mightily into this repercussion, a consequence that will glean for our country an inconceivable destiny. We must join forces, join the solitary commitment this man has sworn to his country. Ladies and gentlemen, please welcome the grandson of General Laurent de Gauvion Saint-Cyr, Laurent de Gauvion Saint-Cyr the Second."

Uneasy chatter filtered through the room. Laurent stood and snapped a salute toward the major and then to the audience. They applauded, and he was relieved and moved by their accord. Later, he would give Major Miller his copy of Hitler's book, Mein Kampf. It would reaffirm the truth about Hitler.

Major Miller returned Laurent's salutation. He gestured for silence and continued his speech. "And now, Father McConnell will lead us to the benediction, after which we will dine. I have a special treat for all of you later in the evening, but for now, let us pray."

**

Christina Cross squinted into the spotlight. Senator Liam Caradine stood in the wings, studying her. She was standing straight and proud, smiling at the audience. Her white gown, inlaid with streams of coruscating gold and silver, was beautiful. The Belgian lace bodice revealed the curves of her porcelain bosom, and her luminescent black hair was swept to one side and held by a magnolia blossom.

79

He thought of the frightened little girl he had comforted so many months ago. The haunting look of hopelessness went to his heart. There would never again be a day as long as that one.

She was still apprehensive and unsure of herself. Her eyes held loneliness, an emotion he was all too familiar with, but he admired her courage to carry on, her mind always busy working, trying to validate herself, sorting out the worry and fears she carried for Nicolette. He would continue to guide and protect her for a long time. He wished he could have done the same for his own daughter.

The conductor nodded and Christina bowed her head, silently effectuating the words to the song. The first and second stanzas sifted through her mind, the key of C planted firmly in her memory, and then, for a frightful moment, she panicked. The third stanza was not there. She quickly went over the beginning, hoping it would jog something. Her brain hunted and probed, and for what seemed dozens of times, she ran the words repeatedly but came up empty.

Her recall was hopelessly gone as if she were in some other time and place. Was father trying to tell her something? No, it couldn't be. It was his dream for her to sing. Never would he wish this upon her!

Silence enveloped the room, and she tensed, searching the sea of black tuxedos. Her panic intensified as she realized Liam was nowhere in sight. The sounds of the orchestra filled the ballroom. She gaped at the conductor and shook her head futilely from side to side, her cheeks burning with humiliation.

The introduction continued once again, but there was nothing she could do to shake her memory. Her mind was a vacuum, the world a vacuum, the only audible sound was the pounding of her heart. Row by row, she searched for Liam again, quickly scanning each face. Her eyes settled on a man sitting in the front row who smiled reassuringly. His expression was sympathetic as if he could feel her pain. She was stiff with fright as the orchestra continued its prelude. The man stood and pivoted toward the audience.

"Your American women, they are beautiful!" he shouted. "*Par excellence*, The United States of America!" He removed his hat and swooped into a bow, then swung his hat toward Christina and bowed again.

Christina was speechless as she stared at the tall, handsome man. His face was tanned by the sun, and his thick brown hair and blue eyes contrasted with his white uniform.

The audience burst into applause as he climbed onto the stage and took the microphone. "I would be honored to dance with the *mademoiselle*," he said politely. He turned and appraised Christina's face and downward, then shook his head as if in a dream. The audience went wild.

Christina looked into his eyes; they held an indefinable emotion, something unsettling. His English was broken, but polished. He was French, she thought, perhaps an officer in some Foreign Legion.

He pressed his hand into hers and drew her near and said softly, "You'll have time to think, to recollect your thoughts, yes?"

She pulled away. "I won't harm you. You looked so frightened, I only wanted to help."

"Oh no, no," Christina stammered. "I can't believe this is happening. I don't know what came over me." She felt her pulse race in his hand. "I'll be all right. Just give me a minute."

"Take all the time you need, my sweet."

The conductor swished his baton and held it for a count, and the man drew Christina close again and began to glide her around the stage.

"Who are you?" she asked.

"My name is Laurent."

"Your full name?"

"Laurent de Gauvion Saint-Cyr."

The violins rose to a crescendo and the audience begged for more. His dialect was beautiful, like music, the most romantic name she had ever heard.

Laurent studied her face, feature by feature. He didn't hear her words or the cheers of the crowd. *"Beaux yeux, mademoiselle,"* he whispered.

"I beg your pardon?"

"You are so beautiful," he said. "There isn't a woman in France who could compare to you. You—" His eyes fastened on her moist pink lips, "—are what I have been looking for all of my life."

Christina stepped away, stunned. His eyes grew wild, drinking her up, ruthlessly daring for an embrace, a kiss. He waited, challenging her to go through with it. The audience cheered.

"Please! I must sing. I must sing," she pleaded.

He raised her hand to his lips and closed his eyes, ignoring her pleas. The crowd whistled.

Suddenly, Christina snatched her hand away and contemplated a reprisal. She darted toward the microphone. "Thank you for your patience," she said smoothly. "I must apologize for this evening. I don't know what came over me."

She turned and gave Laurent a withering stare, furious that her voice shook. He stood with a self-satisfied expression and smiled at her, his blue eyes dancing as though amused by the whole event. How dare he, she thought. She strolled toward him, flashed a defiant grin, and took him by the arm. "Please come," she encouraged. "We'll sing a duet. Just you and I."

He pulled away, and she raised her dark brows toward the audience.

"Yes, yes, yes!" they chanted.

Christina delighted at his flustered manner. "Come now," she bullied. "You wouldn't want to disappoint the audience, would you?"

"I know nothing of singing," he said, staring at the floor. "Must you, *mademoiselle*?"

"I'm afraid I must." She took his elbow and marched him to center stage, and he spread his arms, pleading.

"This I cannot do," he begged. "Your ears will be sorry for this."

"Yes, yes, yes!" the audience chanted again.

He kneeled and clasped his hands. Ah, Christina thought triumphantly, I've got him! Him and his boastful assumptions! His face had turned crimson, his eyes wide, and she suppressed a laugh.

"So, we are even," she gloated.

He rose and swatted the knees of his pants. "Yes, *mademoiselle*. What is the American expression—the mitten is on the other hand?"

The audience roared, and Christina extended her hand to him, but the thought gnawed that she shouldn't have let him off so easily. He brushed her hand with his lips, then quickly walked from the stage. She was exquisite, he thought, the raven-haired beauty in the angel's dress. Major Miller was right; his solemn vow not to become involved with another woman had just shattered.

Chapter 9

Christina and Liam entered the reception suite amid sounds of clinking glasses and merriment. She wanted to leave after her performance, to go to her room and be alone with her miserable thoughts, but he had insisted she accompany him to meet some influential people. The room was crowded with dancing couples, and the Glenn Miller Orchestra played loud and lively.

Laurent turned from the balcony and stepped down the staircase, squeezing through the dancers. "Senator, if you please?" He removed his hat and held it to his chest and offered his hand for a dance.

Christina stiffened and looked at Liam. Laurent remained standing with his hat in his hand as Liam nudged her toward him. "No!" she said, suddenly wondering why Liam was giving her so freely.

"Where are your manners?" he admonished.

"I am honored," Laurent said before Christina could reply. He placed his arm around her waist and swiftly glided her away.

"Truly, my heart was in the right place when you had difficulty recounting your song. I have already apologized."

He took a deep breath, his eyes probing her delicate face. "Why can you not forgive me?"

"But I have forgiven you," she said, looking for Liam.

"Perhaps I did carry on a bit, but you have to admit it relieved the tension. I turned a potential disaster into something fun. The audience, how do you say—" He flicked his eyes up and stroked his chin. "—they ate it up. It was all to your advantage. You have won the *affaire d'honneur*, and you need not make anything more of it."

Christina glanced frantically around the room, squirming to free herself.

"Your senator has left," Laurent said.

"Well, you've accomplished your mission. My evening is ruined. Are you satisfied?"

"I envy your senator, Mademoiselle Cross, and I wish—" He shoved his hands into his pockets and looked at the floor. "There is an old saying," he said. "To understand everything is to forgive everything."

"But you don't understand," Christina tried to say politely.

He shrugged and held out his palms. "You are right. Perhaps I don't, but the measure of your concern is enormous for such a trivial act on my part."

She wished he would go away. "What do you want from me?" she cried in exasperation.

He wrinkled his dark, thick brows and offered a shy smile. Christina admitted to herself that he was devastatingly handsome, not her type, but nonetheless, still attractive. The ribbons and silver medals struck a distinguished contrast on his white uniform jacket, and it was plain to see that he was proud of them. Liam wasn't nearly as handsome, but, like father had said, it was the goodness of a person's heart that counted. "I must go," she said, her thoughts once again on Liam's whereabouts.

"We will meet again?"

"Please, I must go."

Laurent slipped his hands up her arms and brought her close again. He bent and whispered into her hair, "I will send a rose for each day that passes without you."

Christina turned and scurried from the room, banishing the thought of the strange fluttery feeling she felt when his face touched hers.

**

Liam rolled over, heavy with sleep. The tap on the door grew louder, and he sat up, slowly struggling out of his slumber. He reached for his bathrobe and wrapped it around himself.

"Please let me in," Christina pleaded.

Liam slid the latch, swung the door open, and then climbed back into bed. Christina tiptoed in and sat next to him. He pitched his head back on the pillow and shut his eyes.

"Please look at me, Liam." Her stomach churned. He was a complex man, so difficult to understand at times, and she was unnerved by his sudden change in mood after she had danced with Laurent. "That man—it was nothing. You left and I went looking for you."

Liam's expression closed her words out.

"Please, Liam. You offered me to him. What did you want me to do?"

"It's a feeling I have."

"About what?"

"About us, you. I worry. He will break your heart into a million pieces. You won't survive his reputation."

"What are you talking about? Laurent and I? I don't even know him. How could you think such a thing?" Then she shriveled inside. "You do love me, don't you?"

"You know I do. You're as close to me as," his voice grew melancholy, "as my own daughter."

"I—I thought differently by now," Christina gasped.

"You what?"

"I thought you loved me—as a woman!"

"Why, I'm old enough to be your father! I'm a retired senator!"

"It doesn't matter! Age doesn't matter," she cried. "It's what's inside that counts."

"Christina, you only think you love me in a womanly sort of way."

"You're wrong! I want your child!"

"You are a child! Listen to me, Christina." His expression lit with affection.

"When I met my wife, I had this feeling."

"What feeling?"

"It felt as if my whole being was filled with her. Every time she looked at me, my heart turned over. My passion for her grew so strong I knew I couldn't live without her."

"What about friendship? Were you friends like we are?"

"We were more than friends. It was as if we were one, our thoughts, desires, and goals in life. It was all there." He got up and walked to the window and watched the crescent moon. "I'll never find that again," he said sadly.

"Yes, you will, you will!" Christina said, aching for him to find her desirable.

"When I'm older, I know you'll feel differently about me. You'll see!"

Liam turned to look at her and confronted his thoughts. "I want to keep what we have together, what we've always had," he said. "I don't want that to ever change. I feel good about myself now. There's a reason for me to live again, and I'm grateful to you for giving me that reason. I only wish you understood."

Christina ignored his words—words full of sympathy, like a father talking to a grief-stricken daughter. He made no sense. She shrugged off her worries, then joined him at the window and looped her arms around his neck, and hung her head.

Her mind was numb, and somehow, through the scourge of ideas round and round in her brain, she was weary of deliberation. She would think about it no more. Sometimes too much conversation muddied the waters. I'll make him love me like a woman, she thought stubbornly. Love like he never felt before. She lifted her head and smiled sweetly. "I'll return for breakfast in the morning," she said.

**

Christina flicked her long black hair over her shoulders and frowned. "I will not accept these," she said and placed the card back under the red velvet bow.

"But, ma'am," the delivery boy pleaded, "I've been paid a month's wages to deliver them, and I've been searching for you everywhere. Please!" He held out the slender white box. "If you don't want them, give them to a friend."

Christina glanced at Liam eating breakfast on the terrace and cunning replaced her anger. "I'll take them, after all," she said, and lifted the spray of roses from the box, inspected them, and put them into a crystal vase. She placed them on the table out on the terrace and began rearranging them.

"I'm assuming those are for your performance last night. I'm sure there are many more to come." Liam smiled.

"No," Christina replied. "They're from Laurent."

"Laurent?"

"Yes. Perhaps he thinks more of me than just a mere acquaintance—perhaps a woman."

"Christina, if you're trying to make me jealous, you'd best forget it. You know how I feel about him, and you'd better take heed, or you'll suffer some bad consequences. Trust me."

"And what might that be? Friendship? Someone who cares? Someone who might even love me? I'd be downright ignorant not to suffer the consequence. I am not going to end up alone, a withered prune of a spinster, sitting in a rocker till the day I die. I'll take my chances, however terrible they may be."

Liam stood and offered a chair. She ignored his gesture and slid a rose from the vase, then twirled it between her fingers. "I'll have no more lectures," she admonished. "Please, Christina, I'll always care for you and Nicolette, no matter who comes into your lives. I've done everything to see that Nicolette is safe and taken care of. Your mother has no qualms about accepting my money and the services of my staff."

"You're my only family and you must understand. I don't want you to be foolish and reckless regarding your future. I want you to think, use your head, and not be so impulsive. Use good judgment with every decision you make, it'll minimize your pain. Leave plenty of room in your heart for forgiveness, understanding, and love. Life always gives back what you put into it."

"Why are you telling me this?"

"I speak as a father. You've changed in these past few days, and I feel I'm losing you." He stood again and threaded his fingers through her shimmering black hair. He stepped closer and held her face in his large hands. "You're growing up, and someday a man will come into your life. A man who'll fulfill you in ways I can't."

"Never, never, never!" Christina broke away. She felt uneasy, it was an uneasiness she couldn't ignore. She felt isolated from him somehow. Couldn't he understand she needed him—that he needed her? She knew there would be a change. She was growing older, becoming independent, but she had hoped he would see her for what she was and accept it.

"In time, you'll understand," Liam said compassionately. "Youth is impatient, and old age is wise. I would give Heaven and Earth if there were a way to put my head on your young shoulders. Please, let's talk again this evening, perhaps at dinner. By then, you'll have had time to give my words some thought."

Christina shrunk at his dismissal and pouted. She was consumed by impatience and itched to think of a plan that would win him over. Perhaps by supper, she would have had enough time to think of something. She drew her pout into a smile and felt happy again.

**

The evening air was cool, and the mist settled, muting the burnished leaves on the maple trees bordering the cadet dormitories.

Christina leaned against the terrace wall and wrapped her lace shawl snugly around her shoulders. She had practiced her diction and carriage with a book on her head in front of the looking glass; after a while, it reflected her objective. She swept her hair up with silver-backed combs and strategically pushed hairpins in. Carefully, she applied cake mascara, powder, and rouge to her lips, then stepped into a black silk chemise.

She had a long chat with her hand-mirror. To be a woman took practice. It was her intent to be seductive, and now that she felt comfortable, she could execute her desires flawlessly. The glory of West Point spread before her view, and her imagination recounted the likes of Robert E. Lee, Ulysses S. Grant, and Stonewall Jackson sitting tall and stately on their giant stallions, cantering through the entrance gates. She wondered if they would have thought her a woman.

"It is, indeed, a sight to behold," a voice spoke softly over her shoulder.

Christina flinched, startled at the accent, and turned to face Laurent. "Oh, you," she said irritably and swiveled around again.

Laurent shrugged off her look of disdain and continued to speak. "Something has changed about you." He walked around her, then withdrew a handkerchief and dabbed a circle of cake mascara from under her eye. "You are all grown up this evening—*en grande toilette*," he chuckled.

Christina snatched the handkerchief and threw it to the floor. She felt like scolding him but thought better of it when she saw Liam enter the room. He was dressed in a well-tailored black suit and trousers with a starched white shirt and black bow tie. She summoned her sweetest smile, then casually turned and looked toward Laurent and batted her eyes. He watched her expression glow with devilment.

"Yes, West Point is quite a sight," she suddenly chatted to Laurent. "Imagine the history, the famous people who actually stood right here, right where we stand now. It's incredible!"

Laurent smiled at her tone. He had laughed at her clown face; a clear attempt to appear mature, but now he understood, and he was tempted to play her game. *"Oui,"* he replied, "I am surrounded by history where I come from also, and not a day passes that I do not think of my forefathers and what they have accomplished. They have helped make France what it is today."

"You must be proud," Christina purred, "to be part of such a heritage."

"I plan to continue that heritage to help keep France strong and independent."

"The newspapers say there won't be war, but I hear rumors. Is it true? Is it true what they say about Hitler? That he's preparing Germany for war?"

"Your newspaper owners fascinate me. Their foreign correspondents are replete with delusions. Hitler has openly violated the Versailles Treaty, a sure sign of war, yet no one is concerned." He watched Christina's eyes flick toward the senator, then back at him. "But talk of war is not why I'm here. I would like to see you again before I leave for France."

Christina sensed his urgency, and the thought of Liam's reaction excited her.

"When do you leave?"

"Tomorrow, unfortunately. Perhaps we could meet at the salon later this evening."

Christina's heart fluttered. It was perfect. "I'll await your presence. Oh, the roses," she added in a beguiling voice, "a woman couldn't ask for more. Thank you."

Laurent smiled at Senator Caradine, tipped his hat, and left the room. Christina sat at the dinner table, her eyes fixed on the candle flame. Her long, slender fingers traced the rim of her crystal goblet while she skillfully calculated her thoughts. She loved Liam. When would he ever realize it? She watched the play of light from the candle reflect in his eyes, and her imagination piqued at the thought of becoming his wife. She would have him, and nothing would stop her.

"Christina, you look radiant this evening," he said, then waved the sommelier toward them. "You look different— older."

She casually twirled a tendril of hair and smiled dreamily. "Why, thank you, that's quite a compliment coming from you."

"You sure know how to hurt a guy." He nodded at the sommelier. "A bottle of your finest champagne, please."

"I've heard glorious things about champagne," Christina said, excited about drinking her first glass. "Is it true? Does it bear your soul?"

"If you drink enough of anything, it'll bare your soul." Liam laughed. "There's a saying: *in vino veritas.* There is truth in wine."

The sommelier appeared and poured the champagne.

"It sparkles like diamonds." Christina giggled.

Liam raised his glass and clinked it to hers. "I hope you know how much you mean to me."

"And you," she smiled, "will know what it is to love a woman again." She leaned into the table, eager for his response, but his expression grew somber.

"I doubt I'll ever let it happen again," he said. "I can't seem to let go."

"I know what it is to lose also," Christina said frantically. "The emptiness—it fills your soul. And the weariness of life, of having to live another day without the comfort of love, those feelings flooding like a river gone mad. A heart broken, empty of life, abandoned and lonely like so many wilted flowers along the roadside." The words spilled from her lips, her mind ticking on steadily, contriving a way to his heart. "Let it go," she pleaded. "Release it. Love will happen if you let it in."

Liam observed the hopeful shine in her eyes. "And I suppose you'll help me," he said in exasperation.

"Yes!" Her heart leaped.

**

Christina drummed her fingers on the salon bar. She felt lightheaded and everything seemed to be floating. It must have been the champagne, delicious but lethal. Liam had grown increasingly silent during dinner. It was as if he hadn't understood a thing she had said. Convincing him they were more than friends was going to be a formidable task. She eyed Laurent entering the salon and suddenly regretted that she had sensationalized her plans with him to Liam. Liam only seemed concerned in a fatherly sort of way, which frustrated her even more.

"I am most honored you are here." Laurent smiled and sat down next to her. "I was not sure when you would be finished with dinner. I looked in the dining room once or twice. You seemed unhappy."

"It was nothing, really," she said.

"Well, you are much too beautiful to be sad." He nodded at the bartender. "Courvoisier, two, please."

"I've had too much already," Christina said.

"Please, just one—one for friendship."

"All right, I suppose. What could it hurt?" Perhaps if she drank enough of the damned poison, it would kill her, she thought miserably. Suddenly, she felt as if a feed sack had just been pulled down over her. She wanted to forget the whole evening and all of her stupid conniving.

Laurent swirled the amber liquid in his snifter. *"Affolé,"* he said and raised his glass to her.

"Sounds sinful. What does it mean?" She swirled a splash of her drink onto the bar.

"It means you are all I think about. Are you sorry for that?"

She settled back on the barstool and sighed, impatient with worry, the same old questions gnawing. She was sick of agonizing over Liam. "No," she said boldly.

Laurent gently placed his hand over hers, and a tingling feeling gripped her stomach. She gulped the brandy. It felt like fire, burning, choking down her throat. She coughed into a spasm, and her eyes teared, the mascara running in black streams down her face.

"Are you all right?" he asked, reaching over to blot her cheeks with a napkin.

"The brandy, it's very potent."

"Yes," she sputtered, "I am fine, just fine." She was miserable, drunk with worry and alcohol. Her head began to spin, and she felt herself float above it all, seeing things with sudden clarity. She had borne the worst, and life had left her childhood behind. Tonight, she was a woman and was ready to be treated as such. She waved for another drink.

"Please, no more," Laurent said. He stood and closed his hand gently on her arm, and she swung around and buckled to the floor. He quickly lifted her into his arms.

"I don't know what's come over me," she said sadly. Her plan had failed miserably, and all her fears swept back upon her, making her heart thud with a dull, slow ache.

"The brandy is more powerful than it looks," he said sympathetically.

She felt like crying. "Please, I just want to go."

Laurent opened the door to her hotel room and placed her on the bed. He released the combs that held her hair, letting it tumble down around her face. She felt the movement of his breathing, moist and warm against her. His steel-blue eyes were startling against his bronzed skin. This feeling, it was strange, she thought. It was like nothing she had felt before. She closed her eyes and puckered her lips, but he stepped away.

"Sleep well," he said and backed out the door. "I'll call on you tomorrow before I leave."

Chapter 10

Christina tossed her suitcase onto the bed, unpacked, and scurried around, putting everything back in its place before turning on the radio. It was good to be back. The Glenn Miller Band was playing and her thoughts went to Laurent, the strange feeling she had felt, and stranger yet were his words when he had left for France: *"Les jeux sont faits, Christina."*

She traced her lips with her fingers, feeling all those emotions again; his firm, warm mouth pressed against hers as he stole a goodbye kiss on the veranda. She had felt contempt for the overly handsome man, but then this feeling took over, a wayward desire, and it had startled her. She felt at ease with Liam, and it was good to be back with him. Nicolette was close by, and that also gave her comfort, even though mother had forbidden her guardianship.

Liam kept track of Nicolette's comings and goings. He encouraged her mother to keep her in school and saw to it that the family had everything they needed. It was wonderful, the way he loved and cared for Nicolette, but the ache without her was settling hard, and she knew it wouldn't be long before she did something desperate to take Nicolette back from Marguerite.

Liam would resist, but she hoped he would understand. He was stable, his love wrapped around her like her tattered baby blanket, a haven in which she could rest her burdens and feel safe. All she thought of was how much she loved him, everything from the sparkle that lit his eyes to his large square hands, long sturdy legs, and Southern charm.

She loved his laughter and silences and even his impatient shrugs. If only he would love her as a woman. She sat on the bed and listened to music. Moonlight streamed across her as she lay down, too exhausted to take a bath and put her nightgown on. Soon, Liam would see things with new eyes, she thought.

Soon, he would kiss her, and then never minister to her as a child again. Persistence was the key, she thought, just as she had risen above her sorrows and faced life square on. She had taken the worst of fate and conquered it. Surely, he saw the revelation within her spirit. She rolled over, so tired of thinking, and tried to sleep.

The music stopped and a voice broke over the radio: "Germany is closing in on France's border."

Christina sat up and turned the volume dial. It was happening, she thought in disbelief. Just as Laurent had said. There would be war, Munich had destined it. All of his plans to which she had listened to half-bored were suddenly clear. Christina thought of her father and his nightmares. He had seen war, his parents slaughtered like cattle and their village burned to the ground. Germans-father had known them well. Power eluded them once, and their defeat had only stung them to an obsession that went beyond the confines of reality. Power would never elude them again.

She sat thinking, wondering, and feeling sick at the helplessness she felt.

**

Liam picked at his food with his fork and then slid his dinner plate aside. He couldn't believe what he was hearing.

"Someone has to do it!" Christina said desperately. "Mother's drunk most of the time, and Marcel is no better. What kind of life is Nicolette going to have? I know you've done everything in your power to help, but I won't have her living with mother anymore! Believe me, I have thought this through, and it hasn't come easy. I've spent many a sleepless night thinking of a way."

"But it's kidnapping! You heard your mother!"

"She won't find us; we'll be in Europe. You know how important Nicolette is to me and what I've been through. I cannot bear another night lying in bed wondering what she is thinking; if she hurts, if she cries out in her dreams. I hate mother for what she's done. She's put Nicolette in harm's way just to hurt me. Taking her away will certainly be worth my crime!"

"But Europe? Have you gone crazy?"

"My decision is made! I can do something about the war effort and get Nicolette out of the country at the same time. Don't you see? It will work!"

Liam stood and pounded the table with his fist. "Christina! Europe will be torn to pieces! It's no place for young girls. Do something about the war effort at home if you must!"

"No!" Christina implored. "It's not enough!" She felt something desperately tug at her. She believed in her hunches, and the timing was right. Somewhere in the last few days, she left her girlhood behind, and Liam could no longer mold her to his liking. She would join the war like her father had and his father before him.

"Destruction, killing, and rape are what you'll face. I can't let you do this; but, most of all, I will not let you do it to Nicolette!"

"I'm of legal age, and you have no claim on me. I'm going and will suffer the consequences."

Liam's voice trembled when he told her not to go, and his finger pointed and shook at her.

She hadn't realized until now how desperately she needed to go. "I've been in contact with my grandfather, Philippe Pétain. He has always been sympathetic to our situation and would do anything to help us. He has already arranged to bring us to Paris. I would be a fool to refuse him."

Liam sat stunned, not believing the lengths she had gone to plan every detail of her departure from him. "I don't think I could bear it," he pleaded.

"I'm going. It's the only way," Christina said desperately. Liam's helpless expression tore at her. "It's a chance for me to do something with my life, something worthwhile, and most importantly, I will finally have Nicolette. Mother and Marcel will be passed out by nightfall. By morning, we will be long gone. You won't change my mind!"

She thought Liam would see her differently now, independent of him, making a life for Nicolette and herself, growing up. She knew she had hurt him terribly, but the war had changed everything, and she couldn't shut out the thought that he would have done the very same thing had he been her.

**

Nicolette wrapped her arms around Liam and said goodbye. He picked her up and kissed her little red cheeks. "I love you, my princess." His voice broke.

Christina drew forward and hugged him. "Someday, I will make it up to you, all the pain I've caused. I only want a chance to prove myself to you that I am no longer a child with silly dreams and desires. I need to rid myself of the ugly memories: the sounds of sobbing and drunkenness and hatefulness and the way it dragged itself on for much of my life."

"Please understand, or a part of me will surely die. This isn't goodbye, only to the memories that will haunt me if I don't do this. I'll write you every day, and when I have made peace with myself and Nicolette is of age to be on her own, I'll return."

Liam stared helplessly at Christina, and then at Nicolette. He choked down the barrage of pleas and bargaining he had rehearsed. All he could manage was a simple declaration: "You'll never know the kind of love I hold for both of you." His voice broke again. "Godspeed, my girls."

The trample of feet up the stairs to the train platform swept them apart. Christina took Nicolette's hand and weaved her way toward the train. A voice shouted, "All aboard!"

A throng of people crowded onto the platform, saluting, shaking hands, and hugging loved ones. Christina and Nicolette entered the rail car and pressed their noses to the window and waved their handkerchiefs. Liam stood on his toes, searching, straining to find their faces.

Slowly, the windows passed one by one until the train grew small and soon was gone. He traipsed over to a bench and sat down, trying to comprehend the whirlwind of everything, to choke his anxiety. He clutched at his chest and rolled onto the ground. People in the station moved around him, and he looked up at their faces and struggled to tell them to stop the train, but soon their concerned expressions faded into darkness.

Chapter 11

Philippe Pétain made arrangements to meet Christina and Nicolette at the Arc de Triomphe in Paris at a rally honoring him for his promotion to vice-premier. They weaved hand in hand through a swarm of people gathered under the gray stone arch, then edged their way toward a portable platform erected in front of the tomb of France's Unknown Soldier. The mob was quiet: a mixture of ordinary people and soldiers dressed in dark green fatigues with rifles slung over their shoulders. Philippe stood and waved his nieces forward, and they quickly climbed the stairs and stood by his side.

"Christina!" He smiled. *"Et la petite Nicolette!"*

"Yes! Yes! Grandfather," Christina said excitedly.

"It's good to see you, at long last." He kissed each of their cheeks and then motioned to the chairs beside him. "Please sit down. We will talk soon, yes?"

Christina sat tall and listened as he addressed the crowd. He had only visited America a few times and was always impressed with Christina's singing ability. He wrote letters regularly, but when Marguerite no longer wrote, Christina continued the correspondence.

He was a military hero who had fought during the Great War commanding the French forces defending Verdun. He became a Marshall and was elected to the French Academy and was serving as ambassador to Spain when he was called home to become vice-premier.

Christina listened intently to his speech, struggling to recall what little of the language she knew. He began to speak loudly, sometimes shouting, as he directed his wide-eyed stare at certain people. Soon, his words came with difficulty, as if it pained to speak them. She watched the expressions on the faces in the gathering, and their eyes were questioning, reflecting fear and uncertainty. Then they raised their fists and shook them.

"*À bas Hitler! À bas Hitler!*" they shouted. "Down with Hitler."

Grandfather shot his arm up and spread his hand in a gesture of peace to silence them.

"*À bas Hitler! À bas Hitler!*" they shouted louder.

He paced the stage, continuing the gesture until he was helpless to silence them. He waved Christina and Nicolette toward him, and they hurried down the stairs into a waiting Daimler. Security guards slammed the doors and cleared a path for their departure.

"I'm sorry," he apologized. "I'm sorry you had to witness such an ugly scene."

He removed his hat and dabbed at his brow. "I sent you a telegram to warn you. In the last few days, it has become a boiling pot of hostility. The anticipation of war brings out the worst in people. They are restless and unsure of themselves, but you are here now, and I am glad you are safe. Let's try to keep it that way."

He looked thoughtfully at Nicolette and smiled. "You look like your mother, little one."

At the mention of their mother, Christina struggled to restrain herself from crying out the whole horrible story again. Instead, she listened while he settled back into his seat, closed his eyes, and began to reminisce.

He talked at length about his happy childhood in Paris, the fallen blossoms of the chestnut trees, and the tricolor ribbon of silk he had strung them with for his sister's sixteenth birthday. He spoke of the chestnut vendors who poured hot nuts into newspaper twists and Sunday drives in his father's Victoria along the Champs-Elysées. Christina sat silently, relieved she had not spoken ill of her mother, for he seemed a man shortchanged of happiness.

"Look at that!" Nicolette squealed as she watched the children sail their wooden boats in the Tuileries Gardens. Brilliant-colored flowers lined a long path to the central pool, where fountains sprouted in high arcs. "Ain't it beautiful here?" she said, awestruck at the sight. She tugged on her grandfather's shirtsleeve. "Is Mr. Lucky your real name?" she asked. "Pa always said you were lucky."

He seemed twenty years younger when he laughed, Christina thought. His hair had turned silver and his eyes were not nearly as frightening as she remembered. She scanned his ribbons and medals. He looked as though he had accomplished much in his life. "Tell me about the war," she asked. "What does Germany want?"

"Much the same as any country. Power," he said.

"At any cost?"

"Of course," he said assuredly.

"What will you do?"

"I will make no bargains," he said firmly, then took out his pocket watch and tapped the driver. "Colmar, Bourbon Palace, *ventre à terre*." He slid back again and sighed tiredly. "I have a meeting with Parliament. Colmar will drive you to my château. You may unpack your suitcases and rest for a while. I'll be back soon, and then we will see Paris."

The limousine pulled in front of the palace. Tiled steps led to a white-columned entrance supporting a marble carving of the Bourbon family. A statue of Henry IV, the first of the Bourbon kings, stood at the entrance.

"It's beautiful!" Christina gasped. "I've never seen anything like it!"

"I've much to show you, my granddaughters," he said, then opened the door and stepped from the car. "*À bientôt.* I'll see you soon."

The limousine sped away. Christina pulled Nicolette onto her lap and settled back into the soft leather seat. The road wound through rolling green countryside. Snow-capped mountains towered majestically in the distance, shadowing groves of apple orchards. It was Heaven, as sure as she could tell. She thought about grandfather and wondered why father had never liked him. He seemed like such a nice man. She tapped the driver.

"*Oui, mademoiselle?*"

"Do you speak English?" she asked.

"*Oui, anglais.*"

"How well do you know my grandfather?"

"Very well," he replied. "My mother worked for him as a young girl. His *femme de chambre*."

"He's a good man, isn't he?"

He nodded. "My mother loved to sing, so one day he sent her to Paris, to the Conservatoire. She is now a famous singer. *Opera seria*. I owe him much."

She thought of father and how his past had changed him: the interminable regrets, things that ended before their time, guilt for things he had not done or said. She wondered if grandfather fit into father's heart when he died. Christina wondered how things in Paris would change her. She felt without significance, but perhaps the war would change that. Things would no longer be what they had been.

******

Paris was almost deserted. Refuse lay piled and uncollected along the tree-lined avenues. Streets were empty of traffic and most of the stores and offices were shuttered. Christina watched a flock of sheep struggle along the Place de l'Alma. It was strange to see abandoned beasts baaing pathetically as they wandered along.

The Champs-Elysées was lined with beautiful flower gardens, and life seemed almost normal. Parisians walked along its route toward the Rond-Point and abandoned dogs chased ducks waddling through magnificent spraying fountains and flowerbeds. Wind stirred the trees, and a shower of burnished leaves sprinkled over Nicolette.

She ran after them and squashed them with her feet. At the eastern end of the Champs-Elysées was the Place de la

Concorde. Within the huge park were the partial remains of several statues and monuments. The bases had been dynamited and most of the busts were missing.

Grandfather stood quiet and respectful, his head bowed, his hat in his hand.

"This was the statue of General Mangin, my good friend," he said, pointing at the remnants of the base. "He was a French general during the Great War."

"Why is everything smashed to bits?" Christina asked.

"Metal from the busts is supposedly needed for the war effort." He knew the inscription had displeased the Germans. Christina took his hand as they walked toward the Hotel Crillon. Christina thought about the strange indifference of the people they had encountered during the day. It was as if they thought nothing had happened, that the German rearmament was a bluff of some sort.

She watched grandfather scan the hotel. His eyes locked on a window. "That is where France recognized the independence of the United States," he said. "President Woodrow Wilson fought for his Fourteen Points at the peace conference of 1918 in that room over there," he pointed.

It was imminent, he thought, the Nazi flag with its hooked swastika would fly over the palatial eighteenth-century building. In all probability, France's finest hotel would be the headquarters for the German high command. It was clear there would be no defense of Paris, and soon he would have to arrange her surrender.

That evening, they drove alongside the Seine River, following its banks through the heart of Paris. They dined on the Ile de la Cité at one of the few restaurants that had not closed. The café was elegant, decorated in muted gold, with crystal chandeliers and dimly lit rooms. There was no lack of luxury or gaiety inside. Civilian functionaries had the revenue to allocate: Contracts, appointments, the black market, and anything of monetary value was negotiated.

"I feel like a fairy princess," Nicolette said. "I hope I never have to go back home again." She pulled out the fossil from her pocket and showed it to grandfather. "This is my good luck piece. I prayed and prayed every day for Christina to come and get me."

"I am sorry your mother is sick." Grandfather covered his eyes and rubbed them as if to shut out the thought. "Hopefully, she will get well one day."

He watched Nicolette as the maître d' took her hand and sat her at a table. She wore the pink satin dress and white *cloche* hat he bought for her. "You were born to be a fairy princess," he said endearingly.

He smiled at Christina and watched as she fingered the alabaster-colored pearls that had once belonged to his wife.

"I've loved every minute of these past few days," Christina said. "I feel as if I'm living a dream. It must've been hard for mother to leave Paris."

"It was," he said, "but she loved your father."

Christina knew how wildly they fought, so she groped about for some other topic of conversation. "Father was preparing me for the opera. We sang arias every day. I always thought it expressed emotions so much better than words. I love the stories, the passion, anger, joy, and triumph of opera."

"Your father always assured me you had greatness in your voice and that someday you would sing *bel conto*. I am eager to listen again. It has been a long time." The maître d' brought two glasses of champagne and lemonade. *"Un apéritif pour mademoiselle and monsieur,"* he said, and then gestured toward the booth across the room. "Compliments of the gentleman."

Christina turned and watched Laurent smile. Her breath caught.

Grandfather Pétain saw panic in her expression and glanced at the young man.

"I know him!" Christina said. Her eyes darted back toward grandfather. "We met at West Point in New York a few weeks ago. I can't believe he is here. I was singing, and he was in the audience," she said, agitated at the thought. "Do you know him?"

"Yes, unfortunately. We have had many encounters, and I would not doubt that he has followed me here. We are political enemies."

"Oh?" Christina questioned.

"I was educated at his grandfather's academy. They all turn out the same, those men. The same old stagnant ideas on how a government should work. No room for change."

"But I thought you were comfortable with your government."

"It is time for a change; a change for the better. Perhaps Hitler is right. No country will last if we let these Jews run us. Besides, the German invasion of France is inevitable."

"What'll you do?"

"Arrange an armistice."

"But many of your people don't want this. They want their independence." Christina thought about her conversation with Laurent: France was strong and independent and would resist an invasion if it came to that.

"Many of our people are *âmes perdues*, lost souls. They do not know what is good for them. I am most certain there will be a political and social collapse if we don't change our ways."

"But I've heard differently. Hitler's a liar, and he'll continue to lie until he gets what he wants—all of Europe," Christina replied.

"There's much you don't understand," grandfather said as he examined Christina's guileless expression. "You're so young, so very young. I am eighty years old and have already survived a war. I am one of the fortunate ones."

He opened his mouth to speak again, but nothing came, only a lump in his throat. He swallowed. "I witnessed the torture of your grandmother, and I live with that night and day. I will have no more. No more war. Adolph Hitler promised peace and a better government if we comply. I have no reason not to believe him. The German army will protect us from the anarchy of Russian communism."

The shortwave radio had told another story, Christina thought, and she wondered who to believe. She looked at Laurent and the beautiful blonde woman sitting beside him.

"Do you know her?" she asked.

He nodded. "The Duchess of Montrose. A willful child, indeed. It'll be her undoing. She's married and flaunts her conquests like a red cape. That man," he nodded toward Laurent, "was her first love, but he didn't marry her, so she ran off with the Duke of Montrose. It would appear she has the best of both worlds now."

They deserve each other, Christina thought. Liam was right. He was a womanizer, born and bred. They were a striking couple, though. He, sleek and tall; she, blonde and petite. She looked at his face and his bedroom eyes. Too handsome for his own good.

The maître d' approached, holding a silver tray. "A note for the mademoiselle," he said.

Christina slid the paper from the tray and unfolded it. She glanced at Laurent, then back at her grandfather. "He wants to meet with me. He says it is important."

"I'd advice against it. He's trouble for you."

"He says it's an emergency."

"To him, everything's an emergency. He would like to fill your head with his outlandish ideas: the war, his politics."

Christina listened as her grandfather continued to talk. Things puzzled her, unsettled her. Nothing made sense anymore. As the evening wore on, her grandfather's words transformed her logic into frightening suspicions and made reasoning with him impossible. She would have to counter his wishes and meet with Laurent. Perhaps he could answer her questions and calm her fears.

******

It was a day out of the ordinary. Gold and bronze blanketed the countryside, and the air was sweet with Christmas roses. The chestnut trees were filled with snow-breasted nightingales busily reinforcing their nests. A gentle wind fluttered through Christina's hair as she strolled up the terrazzo steps toward the École Spéciale Militaire de Saint-Cyr.

It was the most magnificent château she had ever seen. Leaded crystal prisms scintillated blue, white, yellow, and red in the tall, arched windows as she stepped through a vaulted portcullis and into the great hall. Hardwood floors shone like glass, and old portraits of men in uniforms hung on mahogany walls. An aide escorted her up the winding staircase and into the donjon. He announced her arrival and left the room. Laurent stood from his desk and walked toward her.

"It is good to see you," he said enthusiastically. "You did not mention you would be traveling to Paris." He offered her a chair on the rampart in the garden and poured a cup of jasmine tea. Christina walked past him to the embrasure and gazed out at the sculptured gardens. It was breathtaking, she thought as if she were on top of the world.

"I couldn't believe my eyes when I saw you in the café," he continued. It was a dangerous place to be, he thought. The basement was the meeting place selected by the Resistance to discuss the seizure of the police prefecture.

"I understand you've met my grandfather."

"I was not aware he was your grandfather."

"I'm aware of your differences," she said coolly. "I was advised not to listen to you."

Laurent laughed unwillingly, and his eyes focused on the countryside. "It doesn't surprise me," he said. "But then, you are here; you must have given it some thought."

Christina drew a long, aggravated breath. "My grandfather says it is time for change and that France will be better off for it. He says most of the people feel the same as he does."

"Did he also tell you of Hitler's plan? The kind of government we would live under and his lies to gain territory in Europe? The sacrifices the world would live with? The Jews? People are like sheep, they follow, afraid to ask questions, afraid of the truth, and soon they will follow to the slaughter."

Christina finally turned and intercepted his cold stare. "How do you know so much about Hitler?" she asked.

"It is my responsibility to know. My grandfather found himself at the very same crossroads. He was a patriot. He witnessed the birth of a revolution with the sympathy of a man infatuated with freedom. Wars are all the same, led by men of excessive ambitions. My grandfather witnessed twenty-three years of uninterrupted battles and accumulated sacrifices. France was left in ruins. I won't stand by and watch it happen again."

"Grandfather knows how you think. He'll cut you off."

"He knows it'll be a battle twice fought because our people are divided. There is little time to unify and less time to preserve a sense of France's dignity. There is a meeting tonight. All of our patriots will be there. Those who have abandoned their studies and their professions to form an army. I want you to come to see the truth for yourself."

"My grandfather has witnessed war also," Christina argued. "He doesn't want another. He was tortured and so was my grandmother. Why would he want to re-live that? He is tired of war."

"That is your answer." Laurent smiled for the first time. "He is weary. A tired old man who would like an easy way out. Understand, there is no easy way out. *'Guerre à l'outrance'* is the cry of my countrymen—war to the bitter end. You will understand this and more if you come tonight."

"He is my grandfather, my family, and I trust him."

"I beg you to come, Christina. Come and listen, and then make up your mind."

Chapter 12

Flaming torches reflected the proud, hopeful glint in the eyes of the patriots. They were herded together, shoulder to shoulder, in the outdoor inner-ward of the École Spéciale Militaire de Saint-Cyr. Christina stared at the sea of faces, brave and undaunted, the kind of people who never looked back, who focused their efforts on the task at hand.

It had been a long, spirited night, and by now, she understood their convictions. A sad-eyed man spoke of his family, and how German guards forced him to watch the rape of his wife and daughters. An old woman spoke of seeing piles of dead children in a schoolyard soaked with gasoline, then set on fire.

Hitler had been heard to say to his army, "Close your eyes to pity. Act brutally!" Labor camps had been sighted, and able-bodied men were being worked to death, and the sick were left to die of starvation and exposure or were put to death during mass executions. Others spoke of Hitler's promises to the French hierarchy and their guarantees of wealth and privilege if they surrendered to Germany.

"Conquest," Hitler says, "'is not only a right but a duty.' This is the sickness we face," Laurent spoke through a bullhorn and paced the landing. "It is up to us, my comrades, and we stand alone in our quest. He sent troops into the Rhineland, violating the Versailles Treaty, and no one objected. The world appeases him. Well, we, the Parisians, have appeased Adolph Hitler long enough!"

"He has absorbed Poland, and on this very night, his war machine crushes Denmark, Norway, Belgium, and the Netherlands. In the words of my grandfather, Gauvion SaintCyr, a young man should be ashamed to remain in his room when national independence is menaced! We must absolutely assure justice!"

"*À bas Hitler! À bas Hitler!*" the throng shouted and raised their torches high against the night sky.

Christina watched intently, and the fury in Laurent's voice frightened her. He prowled the landing like a lion surveying its kill, and the color of his eyes had melted to fire. She looked around at the people and thought of their terror. They had suffered hunger, closed dying eyes, and did not know defeat until they died also. She had changed with the passing of the evening. Something had gone from her out of her safe and comfortable world.

Laurent lit a lantern and placed it on the *vargueno* in the salon after the meeting.

"Yes, it is terrifying," he agreed. The dim pool of light illuminated his pained expression. "Their eyes, they tell everything."

Christina shivered. "I remember the same expression on grandfather's face in a photograph taken during the Great War. He commanded the French forces in the defense of Verdun where he spoke his famous words, 'They shall not pass.' He's a man of great sentiment and understanding—a hero."

"He is a hero no longer," Laurent said bitterly.

Christina sprang from the *curule*. "He is! He is!" she shouted. "He knows well of torture and fear, just as your comrades! He does not want war either!"

"Surely you must see! You must see beyond him! He is collaborating with the enemy, hostile to the French Republic, and sympathetic to the dictatorial government of Franco!"

Christina struggled to free herself from his grasp. "Let me go!" she demanded. "Let me go! You don't understand!"

"I understand everything!" he said, his mind a collage of ugly recollections. "And with good reason. You have been in my country for only a few days. You cannot possibly know the ferocity with which my compatriots believe in freedom! This grandfather of yours is a *frondeur,* plotting against the established order of my country. Can you not see that I care about you?"

"Your safety? Your welfare? Do not look so surprised! You saw it in my eyes when we first met. It is—*je ne sais quoi*—an indescribable something between us. Tell me, it is not so!"

His eyes locked her thoughts—perilous, hypnotizing, releasing her soul and drawing her in like the tow of an ocean. His arms locked around her waist, and she felt the heat of his skin through her woolen cape. He lifted her chin; his moist, warm mouth covered hers, and then she pushed herself free of his arms.

"No!" she ordered. "I don't want this!"

"The mind is always the dupe of the heart. You are misleading yourself, Christina. The truth is in your kiss."

"I don't care what you think! I love someone else!"

"He thinks of you as a daughter. It's in his eyes, his expression, and the way he looks at you."

"He doesn't!" She stomped her foot.

"Surely you are not so naïve," he said sympathetically.

"Liam warned me, and he was right," she said. "All the stories are true; you're everything bad!" Suddenly, she wanted to push him down the gatehouse stairs.

"And you believe these stories?"

"You're an international scoundrel!"

"Try as you might to resist, it'll be of little use. Someday, you will surrender." He pulled her into him and forced her lips apart with his tongue and she bit down with flaming anger.

"It's high time someone taught you a lesson," she quivered with insult. "You—you bred-in-the-bone womanizer!"

Laurent moaned and his handsome face flushed with anger.

"Your *acharnement* is impressive," he said evenly. "You should understand something about the French— matters of the heart die hard for us. It is not something we casually toss aside."

"There is nothing to understand about the French!" Christina said slowly, deliberately, flicking her hair over her shoulder. "I have no feelings for you. It's Liam. It will always be Liam, and I hope, for your sake, you'll understand that!"

Laurent could not imagine that such a woman existed. For once in his life, he was inept at handling such a situation. He felt clumsy, bungling every attempt to conquer her. He watched her. She was exquisite. Never was there anyone more beautiful?

He regretted coming on to her so strongly, but there was something feverish he was caught up in, as if an epidemic had swept him up and away. Why was he tormented by what went on in her thoughts? Perhaps it was the way of war and the acceptance of his ephemeral existence, like fleeting shadows in a pine forest. If only he could be certain of just one thing in his life.

**

On June 16, 1940, Philippe Pétain arranged an armistice with Germany and became premier of France. He was now a force in Hitler's war machine, and it came to him that the commandant was studying him carefully like an old master's painting, preparing him for the final plan, the plan that Christina would become part of.

For once, he felt shrewd, brilliant, and lucky. The capital was moved to the city of Vichy, and he was authorized to create a new constitution. Within weeks, he launched a revolution that established fascist political and economic institutions. His government paid heavy financial tribute to the Germans and sent French workers to Germany.

By 1942, Hitler ordered Erwin Rommel and his troops stationed in North Africa to resist Allied landings. He also arranged an opera to be performed for Rommel.

"You should be pleased that the Führer has requested you to sing!" Grandfather persisted. "Did you know that in his youth he sang in the church choir and dreamed of becoming such a singer as yourself?"

"But the *singspiel,* the German opera?" Christina cried frantically.

"The songs are simple, folk-like. You'll have no trouble learning."

"I have only a week before I leave for El Alamein. I can't possibly learn it in a week!"

"The campaign in North Africa is of utmost importance to the Führer! You cannot disappoint him. You cannot let his men down. They are weary of war and need a distraction. I have spoken of your voice to my Führer—that you sing like a bird—and he is anxious for you to sing for them!"

"In other words, I have no choice."

Grandfather shook his head and squeezed his eyes shut. He knew the wrath of Hitler and could not challenge his order. He only hoped Christina could live up to his expectations.

Christina took the box of bonbons wrapped in lace that he had offered and walked to her room. She felt her knees go weak and paced the floor like a stricken animal. It was insane to think she would be singing for Hitler in little more than a week's time. She crawled into bed and tossed and turned all night. In the morning, she got up and walked to the secretary, sat down, and began to write:

My Dear Liam, My letters to you have all gone unanswered. Where are you? Are you alright? I will keep writing for I will never give up hope you are well and happy. Nothing is clearer in my mind than the vision of your sweet face and how much I miss you. War no longer deems me a child, and I worry you will not love me when the smoke of war clears away.

The war has turned brother against brother. It is all so confusing, but grandfather has asked me to trust his judgment. There will be peace and we will be better off with it. We are family and that is all that matters. He founded the French Service Organization, and I am assisting with its production.

Again, do not worry about Nicolette. Grandfather's personal maidservant was with us at all times. I miss you terribly! Please know I love you and I always will.

All my love, Christina

Chapter 13

A cool Mediterranean breeze lulled as the hot, glaring sun ascended over the desert horizon. The roar of a coastal train heading toward Casablanca shattered the morning calm.

Christina sat at the window of a mud-bricked coffeehouse and watched the barefoot Bedouin men dressed in knee-length cotton trousers and skullcaps herd sheep up a narrow, twisting road toward the marketplace.

Corrine Moreau, her maidservant, sat across the table, attentive and concerned, drawing on a cigarette. She was a tiny woman with white hair stretched tightly into a small, braided knot, with red cheeks and ill-fitting dentures that were too large for her small mouth. She had become an endearing friend over the past few days.

"It's not for you to worry, my sweet," she assured Christina. "Fate will decide this war. There is nothing you can do."

"But I can't eat, I can't sleep, I can't do anything anymore! All I can do is dream I'm back home mending the gate on the old fence and nailing the loosened boards on the pigpen and plowing the field for seeding," she rambled. "It's the bombs. The sound is all around us, and I'm frightened."

"The *khamsin* blowing from the Sahara carries the sound. It'll be weeks before they hit. By then, we'll be long gone."

"I wish grandfather hadn't sent us here," Christina huffed. "Desert rats, sand devils, and heat! How could he do such a thing? And tomorrow I am to sing the *singspiel* for Hitler. I am out of my mind with fright. I do not want to sing! I have heard the stories! Why did grandfather do this to me?"

"We all believed Hitler in the beginning," Corrine said, watching her smoke trail to the ceiling fan. "He used psychological warfare to unite and convince his front. His Ministry of Propaganda and Enlightenment censored all the newspapers, radio, books, and all means of communication to increase the effectiveness of his propaganda. His speeches were hypnotic."

"He spoke of world peace, all people living in harmony, no wars, and no worries. He concealed himself and his aims, and it influenced people's actions and thinking. It was later that we heard of the atrocities. We are all sorry now. Your grandfather is an old man, and it was easy for him to get caught up and—"

"And what?" Christina cried resentfully. "He sold out! I tried time and time again to reason with him!"

Corrine gestured for silence and then quickly scanned the small room. "I must trust you." She lowered her voice. "You should know—know everything. Meet me tonight at the Fellahin village in the old district. I will be in the mosque near the entrance. Then I will explain."

Christina could no longer deny her allegiance. She had heard France was unrecognizable: German police, German flags, German confiscation, German press everywhere. France was a unit in the German war machine.

That night, Christina dressed in a dark-colored *galabiyah* and wrapped a cotton veil around her face to protect her from the blowing sand, then scurried along the winding road toward the village. A herd of eland thundered across the desert and disappeared beyond the skyline. Their short, spiraled horns and tufted tails reminded her of the goats back home. They would die, too, she thought sadly. Every living thing was caught up in war.

The old district was crowded with houses, and goats scampered playfully with children up and down the alleyways. She squeezed through Fellahin street singers and dancers, weaving her way toward the white tower of the mosque. Worshippers were gathering in the courtyard, washing their faces and limbs in preparation for prayer.

Corrine stood near the entrance, motioning toward the side door. "Over here," she said, "and keep your face covered."

Christina followed her down the stairs and into the basement. They walked to the *mihrab*, a prayer niche pointing toward Mecca, and kneeled.

"This is the old section of the mosque," Corrine explained. "It's no longer in use." She traced a square with her finger along the floor and lifted a wooden panel.

"What's this all about?" Christina whispered impatiently. "And why all the secrecy? Why couldn't you tell me at the coffeehouse?"

"You'll see." Corrine squeezed through the square and climbed down a rope ladder, then peered up at Christina.

"Come," she waved, "and slide the cover over you."

Christina teetered down the rungs toward Corrine, then removed her veil and peered around. "Where are we?"

Corrine thrust a lantern toward a dark passage. "These are the North African catacombs. They are systems of underground rooms once used as burial places. They form a network of connecting corridors covering about thirty kilometers or so. This passage leads to the coast of the Mediterranean Sea."

Christina peered down the damp, musty hall. The lantern gleamed against bright-colored paintings—figures of the dead with their arms raised in adoration. Graves were cut in the soft tufa rock, and marble slabs closed them in.

Corrine pointed. "These were used for funerals and memorial services. When more space was needed, additional halls were dug beneath the first ones. There, just ahead."

She waved the lantern toward a large opening. They entered a holding room. Christina looked through a small window and saw an oblong table centered in an office surrounded by the French military. Her grandfather was pointing at red circles marked on a map. The grind of generators pumping in fresh air droned over his voice.

"What's going on?" Christina demanded. "He was supposed to be in France! What's he doing here?"

Corrine took her by the hand. "Come over here."

They made their way through another large opening and down a narrow chamber that led to an open cavern. Moonlight flooded through a steep, rocky bluff illuminating an enormous black vessel bobbing on the Mediterranean Sea.

"*Accueil,* Mademoiselle Moreau," a guard said and motioned them up the gangplank. They entered the hull and climbed a staircase to the electronic warfare room. Corrine rapped three times on the steel door.

"*Qui va là?*" a voice asked.

"It is Corrine, Corrine Moreau. I have brought Christina."

The door clanged open and a tall, steely-eyed officer greeted them. "It is best we leave," he said and nodded in the direction of a hallway. He motioned Christina to a metal swivel chair. "Mademoiselle Cross, please wait here. Mademoiselle Moreau will return momentarily."

"I demand you tell me what's going on!" Christina ordered irritably. "This has gone on long enough!"

Corrine smiled a self-assured smile once again and gestured Christina into the chair. "I promise you will be told everything when the time is right. Have a bit more patience, please, my dear. I'll be back soon." She backed out of the door and clanked it shut.

Christina whirled around, exasperated, and tried to think clearly, to find a reason for all the absurdity. She focused on the lights dotting the navigation system and thought of the German submarines, the *unterseebooten,* blockading Britain.

Laurent had said they were the terror of the seas, deadly warships, and Germany had proved their effectiveness as they sank one American merchant ship after another. They hunted in wolf packs, destroying everything in sight. She wondered how this American sub had made it through enemy lines and what it was doing here. It was a monster, at least three hundred feet long.

Moreover, what was grandfather Philippe doing here? What did Corrine want? Her imagination ground to a single conclusion, the only plausible answer she could think of. She had heard of American submarines raiding enemy islands, laying mines in their harbors, and performing rescue missions. It had to be! Liam was here somewhere on this sub and had come to rescue her!

She took a long, deep breath. Everything was going to be fine, and soon she would be home. Home, safe and sound, and she would plan her wedding and move in with Liam, and he would never let her go again.

At long last, she had proven her womanhood and he was coming for her. It was glorious, this feeling she had inside of her heart, and she could barely restrain herself from shouting out in glee.

The door pushed open and Christina whirled around, breathless with exhilaration.

"You look as though you'd like to lynch me and have me dangle from a lamppost." Laurent appraised her stunned expression.

"I—why, I was expecting someone else," she said in disbelief.

"I regret that I have disappointed you. My apologies."

Christina swiveled to face the navigation board. "I thought you had your hands full in France. Surely, you aren't supervising the American fleet as well?" she said sarcastically.

"As a matter of fact, I am." He turned her around to face him. "If you would care to listen, I will explain."

"I would appreciate it, as I seem to be the only person who knows absolutely nothing about all of this," she articulated, then leaned back into the chair and closed her eyes.

Laurent rolled a chair in front of her and sat down. "There are many reasons. Look at me," he demanded.

Christina pursed her lips, waited a few stubborn seconds, and then opened her eyes. "I'd like to know what my grandfather is doing here. Why isn't he advising his fascist government in Vichy?"

Laurent smiled at the contempt in her voice. "You have come to know that your grandfather does not build castles in the sky? That he is a *frondeur*?"

Christina's cheeks grew hot. She hated to admit the truth to such an arrogant, self-filled man and stiffened at his satisfied smile.

He laughed triumphantly. "You have! You have come to your senses, and I am pleased, pleased you now see the truth!"

"You haven't answered my question!" she snapped. "What is my grandfather doing here?"

"He is not here on his own free will."

"You mean you've kidnapped him? Taken him hostage?"

Laurent stood, leaned into her face, and pressed her hands into the armrests. "It was the only way," he enunciated.

"For what?"

"*Bêtise!* Do not act so ignorant! The only way to get information. Information that will save thousands of lives, perhaps even your own!"

"Corrine Moreau? Did she set me up also? How could you? How could you use me like that?"

"Come," he demanded, "I want you to see for yourself. It will explain everything."

He nudged her out of the room and down a long, narrow corridor to the crew's quarters. She stood staring at rows of straw baskets extending from one end of the room to another.

She peered into one and gasped when a tiny, cadaverous child's face looked back at her. She staggered aside and its bony hand reached out and brushed her skirt. The ghastly image whirled round and round as she stepped from one basket to the next, peering in, viewing one horrible effigy after another. She held her hand to her mouth and ran from the room and collapsed against a wall. Hitler's virulence, she thought. It was hell and she was in it. "I have named the operation *Cri de Coeur.*"

Laurent walked through the door. "Cry from the heart. It functions as a human chain, a baby chain to freedom, and if just one link is broken, the operation will fail. It is vital that you understand this."

He rapped the wall with his knuckles. "This is an American sub, and your Major Nicholas Miller is on board secretly meeting with our French Forces of the Interior— the *Maquis*. My father and a handful of others were the only people who knew about these catacombs. He accidentally discovered its existence during the Great War."

"He thought at the time that they were ruins of ancient cities, but after further investigation, he found the chamber was a charnel house filled with the dead. I remembered his stories about this place and knew it had access to the Mediterranean, that it would be conducive for the American sub. The French *Maquis* have been operating from here for three months."

"Where do the babies come from?" Christina gasped again.

"Hitler's *kinderkamps*. We only take newborns as they are not missed, and they fit undetected into garbage pails."

"Garbage pails?"

"There are a few patriots who have infiltrated the camps. They are kitchen workers. The babies are smuggled into the cooking area in large food containers. They are then transferred to garbage pails. The refuse is taken away each evening and tossed into the main dumpsite. Our people hide there, waiting to retrieve only the sacks marked with black slashes."

"The guards—surely they hear their cries!"

"The babies are wizened and starved, much too weak to cry."

Christina peered into the room again and a spasm of nausea gripped her as the horror of it all set in. She felt the sweat on her forehead and steadied herself against the wall.

Laurent reached out and took her hand. "Let me help you down the hall where we can sit and talk. Perhaps you would like a glass of water."

"I just want to run away somewhere," she whispered, "away from the killing and maiming and burning to a place where life has meaning, away from sickness and starvation, a place where you can wake up in the morning and breathe and know that everything is going to be all right," she rambled, then wiped the sweat from her upper lip with the back of her hand.

Laurent guided her into the galley and gave her a glass of water.

Christina gulped it down and then held it with both hands, her head bowed over it.

"So, you're a readymade father." Her voice began to crumble.

"I am alive, their fathers are not." He grew silent thinking about it, thinking about it all.

Christina raised her eyes from the glass and looked into his face, as if seeing him for the first time. "Their spirit is in their children," she said, "and a part of them will live because of you."

"It is the least I can do."

"You're very kind. I never thought that about you."

"I'm well aware of your thoughts. You have never been—how shall I say—circumspect."

"You're right." Christina returned his embarrassed smile. "But I'm sure there are many who think otherwise."

"Yes, I have many adversaries. Colonel Montrose, in particular," he said grimly. "He has thwarted many of our missions and is without compassion. We have a longstanding feud, and he'll stop at nothing to kill me or anyone associated with me."

"Montrose," Christina remembered the name. His wife had been in the restaurant with Laurent the night she and grandfather had dinner. "I cannot blame him for wanting to kill you," she said sarcastically. "You were bedding his wife."

Laurent didn't attempt to hide his amazement at her revelation. "I see your grandfather keeps you apprised of my personal life, as well. That affair has long since died. I am committed to nothing except this war." He said something in French, and Christina watched his expression softening to sadness. He looked like a small, lost child.

At a loss for words, she changed the subject. "What about my grandfather? How much of a threat is he to you?"

"He's collaborated with us on every detail of Rommel's invasion of North Africa. There are times I think he has cooperated willingly, of his own accord. I cannot, however, let his actions cloud my judgment. There is much at stake, and I will trust no one."

"But you trust me."

"It is my job to know whom I can trust and whom I can't. It has taken a lifetime to master rightful judgments."

"I'd like to help."

"What about the French Service Organization?"

"I won't sing for Hitler."

"He will be outraged." Laurent smiled.

It was the word 'liquidate' Christina had heard on the shortwave, and it had terrified her. She could not shake it from her mind, the ethnic cleansing of the world, the German solution to life. She thought of the armies massed on the border.

In her mind, she saw the men, the tanks, the bombs, and the German will to conquer. How much time before, but it did not matter. She had made up her mind, and life was the only thing that counted; if she could save just one child, she could bear the nightmare.

Chapter 14

Laurent arranged for Christina and Nicolette to share a bunk on the second deck of the nurses' quarters in the submarine. Christina plunged into her duties, working shifts around the clock, assisting in medical care, feeding the babies, washing clothes, changing sheets, and administering medication and comfort to the blind, deaf, and paralyzed. She found herself on an emotional rollercoaster. As soon as she nursed the infants back to health, they would leave.

Always a new destination, another surreptitious port. It was becoming more difficult for her to let them go, agonizing over their welfare before she went to bed and each morning when she rose.

"Are they safe when they leave here? Do they go to good homes?" she asked Laurent.

"There are hundreds of *Maquis* conducting intelligence operations," he explained.

"They live in hiding in the mountains of southern and eastern France. The Allies parachute supplies guns, ammunition, and food to them. It's these people who seek their final destination. They wait at selected checkpoints around the coast of Africa for our submarine. We deliver the babies, and they hide them in shelters until they reach the Allies."

"Will they be reunited with their parents?"

"Most likely they'll never set eyes on them again." He studied Christina's expression. "It's a vexing damnation weighing on the souls of everyone," he said, sighing wearily. "All we can do is occasionally save a life—here and there, save a life. It is what sets us apart from Hitler. He is taking and we are saving."

"I wish I could keep them all. No one else understands what they've been through."

"Perhaps it is for the best; it would be too horrifying if they knew."

Nicolette came running with a stack of diapers. "Nurse Liz said I could help change the babies!" she squealed with delight.

Christina took the diapers and placed them on a shelf.

Nicolette shifted her eyes toward Laurent. "Please?" she pleaded. "I really can help!" She reached into her pocket and rubbed her fossil for luck. She had done that a lot lately. It seemed to be a fixation that swept through her when she needed fresh hope.

Laurent shook his head and laughed. "What have you got there?"

"My luck piece." She plopped it into his hand.

He examined it slowly, studying the creature inside. "Well, it brought you luck today. In my book, you are old enough to help those babies." He lifted her up and dropped the fossil into her shirt pocket. "I have a most important job for you. I'm told that you are a connoisseur of lullabies, so

I appoint you to sing every evening at bedtime until the babies fall to sleep."

Nicolette giggled and clapped her hands. "Oh, yes, sir! I can sing, all right! I can sing real pretty for them babies."

"I have not a doubt. You have a fine teacher." He smiled at Christina and found himself wondering what he had missed in his life. Nicolette had captured his heart. Her chaw bacon mannerisms had amused and enlightened all the patriots. They had named her *je ne sais quoi,* and it was rightly so, for she was just that—an indescribable entity.

Later that night, Nicolette came down from her quarters. Through the shadowed mist rising from the sea, she peered at the dark, cloaked figures running down the gangplank handing bundles to outstretched arms. It was time. The babies were leaving again, and it was all she could do not to chase after them. She prayed for courage because Laurent had said that was what it took to win wars. She scampered into her bunk and pulled her blanket over her head.

Someday, she thought, the babies would all come back, every last one of them, if she prayed long and hard enough. Day after dismal day, she prayed, but nothing ever happened. Soon, she realized that they were never coming back. She remained in her bed for days, rubbing her fossil, and making a plan.

"What is it, Nicolette? Don't you feel well?" Christina asked and placed her palm on her forehead. Nicolette rolled over toward the wall. "Please, you can tell me; you can tell me anything."

"Nothing is good no more, ever since—"

"Ever since what, sweetling?"

"Ever since my babies left. I want them back. I want them back more than anything! They need me to sing to them!"

Christina rolled Nicolette over to face her. "Bless your little heart; I should've known how awful this was going to be for you."

"Please," she sobbed, "please bring them back."

"There now, shhh, shhh," Christina comforted. "It's going to be all right. In a matter of days, more babies will be coming. Sure as biscuitroot, you will see!"

"But Major Miller said no more were coming."

"Why, there's a group expected next week."

"No, there ain't; I heard him! I heard him talking to Laurent."

"There, there, now, don't worry. I will talk to Laurent. I am sure there is some sort of misunderstanding. Everything is going to be just fine, you'll see."

Nicolette sat with her chin in her hands and thought. After a while, she began to feel happy, happier than she had been in a long time. Every time she thought of her secret plan, her stomach flipped with excitement.

Laurent paced the electronic warfare room and rubbed his fingers through his thick dark hair. "Nicolette is right, Christina," he admitted miserably. "We are suspending Operation *Cri de Coeur* to concentrate our efforts on Operation Lightfoot. It will take all of our manpower to force the Axis armies out of Africa. We hope to relieve pressure on the hard-pressed Australian forces."

"Your American General Montgomery has begun the second battle for El Alamein. Five hundred troops and supply ships, escorted by three hundred and fifty warships, are awaiting further instructions. We hope to catch Rommel by surprise with as little fighting as possible.”

“But the babies,” Christina moaned. “What will become of them?”

“First things first, we must carry out this mission. It is our only chance to save more children in the future.”

“There must be something I can do!” Christina implored, trying to comprehend what was happening and how it would affect all they had accomplished.

“There is. I hope to persuade your grandfather to order Admiral Jean Darlan to halt the French Resistance to the Allied landings. We must unify all of our forces; it is our only chance to stop the invasion. We will also enlist the aid of the French Navy—it is still capable. I need you to negotiate the plan with your grandfather and convince him. We don’t have time for another long campaign.”

“I’ll try, I’ll try anything, but what if he refuses?”

Laurent drew a deep breath, then looked across the room at Major General Schaffer, studying a map of North Africa. “It will be best for all concerned if you can convince him to do this willingly,” he said in a formidable tone.

**

Christina peered into the holding room. “Grandfather, it’s me,” she said, tapping on the window. He didn’t look at her. “Please let me in,” she said to the guard. The guard opened the lock and then pushed the door open, and Christina stepped inside.

“Grandfather,” she repeated.

He lifted his head and glared. His eyes were etched with dark circles, his face pale and drawn. "It's best you leave," he said. "I have nothing to say."

"But, grandfather," she pleaded, "we must talk. It's very important!"

"You're nothing but a traitor, my own flesh and blood!" he said, towering over her.

It was extraordinary to realize she had once been in awe of him and how quickly everything changed. She felt numb and battered by the suddenness. "I can't believe you still don't see the truth!" she stormed. "How can you ignore the poor, sick newborns that fill this place? Surely their cries keep you awake at night!"

"You know very well what my position has been. I have been kidnapped, made to choose between you and my Führer, and you have been duped. As for the babies, there are children starving everywhere in this world."

"You've stuck your head in the sand long enough!" she cried, impatient with his rationalizations. "You had hoped that Hitler would just go away, disappear, that he was bluffing, so you appeased him. Well, he is not going away! He is here to stay, and he will murder anyone who stands in his way. Please, grandfather, can't you see? You must help or we'll all die!"

"There will be a better France, a better Europe, and a better world. There will be peace. Hitler has promised this, but you do not believe it, so there is nothing more to say."

"Peace? Triumph without war is more like it!" she shrieked. "Germany today; tomorrow, the world—the slaughter of our own blood. Why aren't you outraged?" She thought of the children that would die and how they would die. The Germans would march everywhere, anxious to avenge themselves.

"It's the price of war. I've seen it all of my life. It's nothing new to me."

"You must help, or—"

"Or I will die? I am a dead man, anyway; you have chosen not to sing for my Führer." He clutched his chest in a coughing spasm and then took a kerchief from his pocket and spat into it. "It is just as well," he wheezed, "for I am tired of life. My business on earth is finished. My wife, my children, and my friends are all dead."

"But what of Nicolette? Of me?" Christina cried, aghast.

"This war has made me a soldier. It has taught me fidelity in duty and swiftness of decision. I have molded many a mutineer to discipline, and the soldier dedicates himself, absolutely, when he has faith in the certainty that his general will never engage uselessly or sacrifice him. France faces the situation, in fact, and she does not hear danger knocking at her door; she listens to duty and to pride, and you would do well to do the same. Patriotic enthusiasm is completely necessary to the health of France."

"You're a stubborn and foolish old man! You are primed to commit the sin of all sins, the sin of causing pain and death to others!" His expression changed as if he knew something she did not. "What?" she asked.

"Your words are an echo from my past."

"I don't understand—"

"*Ça ne fait rien,*" he said. "You must go. Off with you!"

He pushed her out beyond the door, and she shouted, "God in Heaven, you must listen! You must listen to me!"

He shut the door, then sat on the cot and stared at the floor. It began again, thoughts filtering through his tortured brain: doubts, fears, pleasure, and ecstasy. Coiled, twisted gusts dissolved in a world possessed by fantasies, by devils. The fire of malaria began its pestilence, and he braced himself for another convulsion.

The days were shortening, and he wondered when he would die. He guessed that the pinnacle of life was death, for it was only then a man saw his existence for what it was.

He moaned, concentrating on his agony. He thought of his daughter and his son, he thought of Christina, Nicolette, of children, and how they showed their souls honestly among themselves. They gathered kindly, reticently, and talked passionately about what they desired and felt.

Adults were not like them; he was not like them. He was knowledgeable and maneuvered for rank, countering for power no matter the cost. There were too many theories, hypotheses, ends in themselves, things that scattered the mind and left no room for honesty, things that became meaningless when placed beside the endless tide of an ocean. He wished he had been a better man, and he prayed for time. He was in a position now to undo the hideous wrong.

Christina collapsed into her bunk, weary with fear, drained of strength and energy. Never had she known such a deluge of emotion beyond her power to understand or explain. In her mind, she heard the thunder of guns, the best and the strongest of the German race, their columns marching rhythmically, boots stomping African roads, fighting, and killing.

She dared to think of Operation Cri de Coeur. The die was cast. A country would be reduced to rubble by the act of a single man.

She hated her grandfather. How well he had stated his case! How well he played his part! He was no more than a pawn caught up in the blueprint of a madman! There was something about his expression, the way in which he had dispensed his words. It was odd, she thought, and ran them over and over in her mind until she lay back in exhaustion.

She couldn't sleep and turned from side to side trying to shut out the past few hours, but her grandfather's words went on piercing her thoughts like bullets through a tin can. She lay on her back with one hand under her head and stared up at the domed ceiling. She felt hollow and alone, so terribly lost and without direction. She sat up and hugged her knees and a piece of paper flew out from beneath her pillow. Nicolette's printing leaped at her:

Deer Kristeena,
I hav gon to find them babees.
I wil be bak soon.
Nicolette

Christina rolled from the bed, stunned, her worst fears realized. There were a hundred places Nicolette could have gone. If only she had thought—it was so like her. She ran from her room and down the gangplank. Soldiers passed by, and she pleaded for help. They snatched lanterns, formed groups, and foraged through the limestone chambers frantically calling out Nicolette's name. Minutes soon passed into hours and Christina forbade herself to weep, for if she began, she might never stop.

What hope was there for Nicolette, or anyone, she thought. It was no longer a sane, ordered world, and now she felt she was on the verge of madness.

She climbed the rope ladder, pushed the floor panel up, and climbed out. A flaming shaft tumbled before her into a ball of fire. In a daze, she wandered around the flames, dodging them here and there until she left the mosque. She stood shivering outside, staring in disbelief at the ashen ruins surrounding her, seeing nothing, seeing everything.

It caught her eye suddenly; clean and white in the midst of the black smoke dangling from a pile of twisted metal. She ran across the courtyard and snatched it. Dread choked her as she registered two little blue buttons hanging grotesquely from the face of Nicolette's sock doll. "God in Heaven, no!" She clutched it to her breast. "No! No! No!"

Frantically, she searched the periphery of the ruins, her thoughts lost to Nicolette.

The pain of the unknown began.

**

Cool rain teased the hot, parched desert, and out of the dawn charged a white stallion racing against the wind. He halted and reared back on his legs. His eyes were black and wild, hypnotizing Christina as she stood frozen in her tracks. The sky grew dark, and lightning bolted quickly toward her.

Father whispered and warned her, but a limba tree tumbled over and pinned her to the ground. Suddenly, the sun pierced the cataclysm and calmed the sky, and the black clouds dissipated into a glittering rainbow. The stallion disappeared as if carried off by demons into the howling squall, and in his place was the cuirass Father had worn as a mounted soldier.

Christina sat up, struggling to drag it near. Wildly, it began to spin, first clockwise, then counterclockwise, and then it lifted into the air and hovered over her, flickering as the sun struck its gold. Suddenly, it dropped before her, and Nicolette rolled from it into her arms.

"Nicolette! It's you! It's really you!" she squealed in disbelief. "Father! You sent her back to me! It was you, it was you—" A hand caressed her cheek, and she pressed it with hers.

"There, there, my sweet," a voice said tenderly. "Please don't be frightened; you were having a bad dream."

Christina focused on the face. "Father sent Nicolette to me, and we're going home where we'll be safe," she said hypnotically. "It'll be just like old times—picnics by the river, picking berries for preserves, and fishing for buffalo fish."

She pulled the coverlet to her face and inhaled a mélange of Nicolette's child-scents, and it became suddenly real. All of that had gone and with it, hope, belief, and all the things that made life bearable. She buried her face in Laurent's shoulder and sobbed.

Laurent saw a whole new image of war. In his brain, pictures gyrated of Nicolette, and he could not bring himself to spill his guts, to tell Christina about the struggle of routed *Maquis* who had witnessed the Nazis take her away. The next day, they had returned with a regiment headed by Colonel Montrose and had leveled the mosque.

Laurent could feel it bearing down on him now; every muscle and nerve tightened into knots of revenge, and he could taste the sick rage that left him gasping, and suddenly, the war paled to insignificance. He would find the murderous swine, Colonel Joachim Montrose, seek him out like a lion seeks its prey cunning, savagely, and then Montrose would wish he had died in his mother's womb.

Tanks battled in the fierce desert heat. American, British, Australian, and French *Maquis* stormed the Axis lines armed with rifles and *kukri* knives. On November 5, 1942, bagpipes and bugles broke under a full moon. The Axis lines at El Alamein had been broken. Hitler immediately ordered his troops to occupy France and skin Philippe Pétain alive.

Chapter 15

Young boys worked as loaders and haulers in the endless maze of suffocating coal shafts. The coal was hauled by buckets to the preparation plant, where it was sorted, washed, and dried. From there, it was loaded into unit trains and shipped to Axis ports scattered throughout Europe.

The *kinderkamp* had been christened the 'Devil's Palace', a surreal hodgepodge of iron and concrete dormitories surrounded by barbed wire.

Nicolette huddled on a concrete slab, her arm wrapped tightly around Marie, a tiny, olive-complexioned girl with a crippled leg. "Soon as we get outta here, we're gonna turn into fairy angels, sure as biscuitroot," Nicolette whispered to Marie. "So's best you try to be quiet and stay out a Bull-Face's way so she won't whip you with her cudgel no more. If you feel the pain coming on in your leg, just holler in here."

She wiggled her sooty fingers and then pressed her hand firmly against Marie's mouth. Nicolette glanced at a spider's web draped across the barred window. "Besides, we gotta take care of Maybelle and Louis." She smiled and watched as the two spiders busily repaired a hole. "Who'll look after them if we're not around?"

Marie peeled Nicolette's hand from her mouth and gasped for air. "Well, we have to take care of Jonathan's spider, too," she said and shook her bony finger authoritatively.

"Why? Jonathan said he wouldn't give George up for anything, not his clay marbles, nothing."

"Jonathan's gone."

"Gone?" Nicolette scanned the huddle of children.

"He went to Heaven yesterday," Marie said sadly. "He broke his coal bucket by accident."

Nicolette looked up at the riprap covering the ceiling. "I wish I was Jonathan," she said wistfully. "Now he's with all of them angels floating around on them marshmallow clouds." Nicolette was sure Christina and Laurent and all the patriots were in Heaven by now. She wept night and day for them. The giant dragon men in their green uniforms were monsters sent by the devil to torture and kill. Their gun machines and firebombs had surely sent them all to Heaven with pa, she thought.

She watched Jonathan's spider crawl toward its web and quickly cupped her hand over it. "Don't worry, George," she said, "me and Marie are gonna take good care of you. It won't be long until we all turn into fairy angels. Soon, you'll see Jonathan again, and Christina, and my pa, and Laurent, and—"

Nicolette bunched her hand small over the spider and contemplated what she must do. Tears filled her eyes.

"What?" Marie asked. "What's wrong?"

"When we get to Heaven," she blinked, "we've got to bring May-belle and Louis with us, and we've got to bring Jonathan his spider, too. So's I expect we'll have to kill the spiders like Bull-Face killed Jonathan. It's the only way we'll ever get them there."

"No!" Marie cried, flapping her skinny arms. "Who says you have to die before you get to Heaven? I was in Heaven before I came here."

Perhaps she was, Nicolette thought. Marie was born of privilege, her parents were of Belgian nobility. She had spoken of royal parties in beautiful castles with mountains of presents and ice cream and cake and elegant silk party dresses in every color of the rainbow with satin shoes to match. Marie was a living fairy angel, she realized. A real, live fairy angel and she had been sent by pa to guide her to Heaven.

She wrapped her arms around Marie and giggled gleefully. "Oh, Marie! I'm so happy you're here with me," she said. "Because of you, we'll all go to Heaven! We'll never be hungry again, or cold, or sick, and we will be with our families, just like before. Oh, Marie, I love you!" Nicolette unbunched her hand and watched the spider scurry to its burrow.

Marie shrugged and smiled a pleased smile. Nicolette always made her feel good, like magic, she thought. That is what she liked about her, most of all.

The weary, bedraggled children wove into each other's limbs and shielded themselves from the icy dawn. Beams of sunlight splashed across their faces as Frau Heinrich opened the door and waved her cudgel toward the containment yard. They rubbed their eyes, blinking sleep away, and slowly adjusted to the sun's rays.

One by one, they unraveled from each other and filed outside. They picked up their buckets and scurried to the bread canisters where they shoved fistfuls of molded crumbs into their mouths and washed them down with tepid *bouillon.*

They were then loaded into caravans and taken high into the mountains to Camp Sturm. On their journey, they peered out between the wooden slats of the trucks at the beautiful, magical land of icicles and icefalls. Glittering snowflakes fell softly like feathers onto oak and beech trees, and they whispered among themselves a fantasy of escaping into the crystal beauty of the hinterland.

Their will for living was waning. It was in their faces, in their eyes, as the Nazi guards shoved them, one by one, out of the convoy and into the coal mine. Marie wobbled behind Nicolette, struggling to keep her stride. The searing ache from the wind paled at the throb of raw, open wounds on her palms from carrying her coal bucket.

Nicolette had torn strips from her shirt and wrapped them around Marie's hands, but the cloth had become filthy, the mixture of rust, coal, and blood aggravating the wounds even more.

Marie whimpered softly and willed her leg to keep its pace, but a guard struck her with his rifle and she tripped. Nicolette stopped, turned, and saw her sprawled against a mine beam. Marie's eyes were closed, her face mottled with gray and blue splotches.

Nicolette ran to the guard and clutched his uniform. "Please, please, help her!" Tears spilled, stripping her dirty cheeks.

The guard shoved her back, but she scrambled to her feet and ran at him again.

"You don't understand!" she yelled defiantly. "She's my fairy angel sent from Heaven, please!" She bolted toward Marie and snatched the coal bucket from her side. "I'll fill her bucket!" She waved it frantically before the guard. "Please, mister, I'll do all of her work and mine, too, just let her be, don't hurt her anymore, please!"

The guard grunted and walked away, but Nicolette ran and fell upon him and reached into her pocket. "Take this, mister, take this!" she cried. "It's my luck piece!"

The guard snatched it and peered at the creature inside, then laughed cruelly and threw it down. She picked it up and wiped it on her sleeve until it shone, and then waved it desperately before him, her eyes pleading, begging for compassion. "It will bring you luck!"

"It has done nothing for you," the guard spoke in broken English. He pushed her aside, and she staggered back onto Jeremiah Ziegler. The whites of Jeremiah's eyes gleamed from his coal-smeared face; his fourteen years masked by his tall, brawny build. He stared defiantly at the guard, then took Nicolette's bucket and threw it with all his might, clinking and clanking across the mine.

The guard rushed at him and wrapped his huge gloved hands around his neck and squeezed until his face turned purple. "The crows will fight over your flesh!" the guard boomed. He released his grip and Jeremiah's knees buckled and he slid down the wall into a heap.

Nicolette stood motionless as she watched the guard pick up his rifle and punch.

Jeremiah's stomach with a force that sent blood spewing up into his face. He grabbed him by the collar and dragged him out of the mine. Another guard trudged toward

Marie and dragged her out, too. Nicolette ran after them and collapsed onto Marie's small, lifeless body. The guard pried her off and dragged her back into the shaft, then dumped Marie and Jeremiah into a wheelbarrow and carted them away.

Nicolette lay crumpled on the mine floor. Her hand tightened over the fossil until her knuckles shone white and she continued to pray. She remembered Christina's words:

"Courage is fear that has said a prayer," and suddenly felt her fright being replaced by something bigger and more powerful than she had ever felt before. She picked herself up and ran from the mine. "Marie, please don't leave me," she cried. It was a blustering hysterical gargle, and the sound of it shocked her.

"I'll never get to Heaven; I'll never get there without you!" And she threw the fossil with all her might.

**

Nicolette clung to the bars in the confinement cell where she sang day after day, racking anguish in the heart of the pacing guard. His face was old and tears filled his eyes just as they had when he had pulled Marie's body from the mine. He reached into his coat pocket, pulled out Nicolette's fossil, and placed it between the bars. She scooped it up and inspected it slowly, carefully holding it toward the light. She kneeled on the floor and whispered a prayer, then crossed herself and stuffed it down into her boot.

"Tis your fate that is in the hands of God now, for you have killed a man. Struck him in the head. Never have I seen anything like it! You are too young to have sinned like that," he said in a thick brogue.

Nicolette shrugged and eyed the sugar cube he had placed before her. She put it into her mouth, holding it against her tongue, letting the sweetness slowly dissolve and trickle down her throat. It jolted life through her body, and she hungrily licked the crystals from her lips, her fingers, and her palms.

"Tis a beautiful song you sing," he said. "Mother sang it to me son when he was born. He's dead, and I have become a traitor." He glanced over his shoulder, then slid his rifle to the ground and rested his arms on the butt. "You Irish?" he continued.

She shrugged again.

"Aye, you have the hair and the skin." He poked his gloved finger through the bars and touched her cheek. "Was the wee girl in the coal mine your friend?" he asked. She nodded. "I am ashamed of this war and what it has turned us into." He lowered his eyes and felt as hollow and lifeless as Nicolette's expression. "A lifetime of mistakes makes us wrong, not wise. We are caught like rats in a trap in the scheme of a doyen's utopian dream."

Nicolette crinkled her brow and stuck her hand through the bars again.

"Ramblin', I am," he continued and placed another cube into her hand. "I am sorry your friend is dead. And I am sorry me son is dead. Your ma? Pa? Family?"

"Dead," she said.

He fingered her clump of matted curls. "One day, my little *acushla*, we will find them all in Heaven, and then it will be as it once was."

He was lying about Heaven, Nicolette thought. He didn't know anything about Heaven. "You're wrong!" Her voice was suddenly strong and sure. "My fairy angel's dead, and now I'll never get to Heaven! Why did he kill her? Why? She never did anybody harm. Why is everyone killing everyone?"

He slung his rifle back over his shoulder and gawked at her emaciated face, at a loss for words, not knowing how or why. "In all the madness, I've lost the reason," he said, thinking about the wisdom of innocence. If only men were more like children, pure, with no harmful motives.

"Why didn't you help her? You could've helped!" she cried.

"One man against an army?"

"Yeah—like Jeremiah!"

"Jeremiah?"

"Jeremiah Ziegler, the boy who helped my friend."

The old guard slouched and kicked the snow. He would never forget that boy. The war would have never been if grown men had believed as that boy had, he thought. All those children had weathered storms and handled stress in the worst of conditions, and yet they could still laugh and play children's games when they were alone. He admired their spirit; never had they traded conviction for convenience. He wondered about his own son, and if he had died with the same courage.

"Your friend is a hero," he said. "The world is made up of people who would like to be like him but haven't the courage. Aye, to die a hero would be a blessing."

A smile flickered and Nicolette reached for another sugar cube. Thirst and hunger soon hurled Nicolette into a cache of fantasies. It was in these dreams she escaped from the grotesque reality into a world of imagined euphoria. She slid down mountains of rock candy into pools of chocolate and skipped ropes of licorice.

The sun shone warm upon her face, and the smell of dew on persimmon blossoms replaced the stench of feces and urine. It was not long before she began to feel she was slipping into the sanctuary of paradise.

One day, the old guard didn't come and in his place, a tall, husky German officer appeared. He looked into the cell, combing it thoroughly until he spotted her huddled beneath the window. She listened as his key entered the lock and the door clanged open. His eyes settled on her, roving from her face to her shoulders and downward. Her heart hammered as he lumbered toward her. He continued his cold stare, unbuckled his belt, and let his trousers drop before her.

"You all right, mister?" She panicked and jumped to her feet. The guard looked startled. She ran as if by an involuntary reaction toward the door, and he grabbed her by the hair and pulled her back, and held her head with both hands. His nostrils flared and his face turned purple, swollen with blood. She hung suspended; her legs and body dangling like a marionette.

Vaguely, she heard gunfire in the distance and somehow it was enough to make her comprehend that she was protected, and suddenly, the man toppled over and pinned her to the floor. Blood oozed from his chest onto her, and she struggled to free herself, kicking, pushing, until finally she was able to crawl away.

She huddled back into the corner, afraid to take her eyes off the corpse. It was big and grotesque as it lay sprawled before her in its vermilion puddle. His eyes were expressionless, blue pellets glaring with an anger she could not comprehend, and she wondered if he had gone to Heaven. Soon, there would be no room left there, she thought, and then she began to cry deep mournful sobs.

Soon, the old guard came and slid the body out of the cell. "Aye, now we have both sinned," he comforted Nicolette. "'Tis easy to make a choice when you have to."

Chapter 16

British and American forces smashed out of Normandy and drove northeast through northern France and Belgium toward the German border. An invasion troop of French *Maquis*, charging from the Riviera up the Rhône Valley and into the small, dreary market town of Bastogne, had captured a German battalion. Shattered German units in the west were regrouping.

Hitler, desperate and filled with retaliatory rage, had calculated a secret counter-offensive. It caught the Allies totally unprepared, and they fought the onslaught against a rival as tough as the Germans—the bitter Ardennes winter.

The French *Maquis* set up headquarters in the cellar of an abandoned farmhouse near Bastogne. A makeshift clinic occupied the main floor. A roving German force had captured most of the medical unit, including several surgeons and equipment.

Christina worked alongside medical corpsmen and Belgian civilian volunteers aiding the few surgeons who were left. With an apron covering her from neck to foot and her hair pulled up with a shoelace she bathed the filthy, bewhiskered men who stank from gangrene and cleaned and dressed their stumps.

Frostbite and trench foot were epidemics. Foot soldiers who broke trails through snowdrifts were exhausted after struggling only fifty yards. Infantrymen who manned the snowy foxholes had chilblains, pneumonia, and dysentery. The harshness of the winter had not been anticipated; their combat gear was no match for the grueling weather.

"Sir, the men are wearing sleeping bags and urinating on their rifles to keep them from locking up, and the wounded freeze to death before we get to them." The despair in the young platoon commander's voice brought the full horror of the situation sweeping down as nothing had before.

Laurent looked from his map, filled with anguish for what he was about to confess. "I bypassed shipments of winter clothing in favor of petrol and ammunition," he said regretfully.

"I gambled, and now they are paying." He had betrayed his men in the name of selfishness, and a war twice fought would destroy them all. He had been assigned a rescue mission: push through Saint-Vith to Schonberg and open an escape corridor for two American regiments of the 101st Division trapped on one of the forested flats of the Schnee-Eifel.

It was more than he had hoped for—his only opportunity to find Nicolette. Philippe Pétain was left with a regiment of the French *Maquis* to hold the former position. The entire regiment had been massacred, and Philippe Pétain was captured by the German high command.

Major Nicholas Miller's paratroopers had discovered the words: *Nicolette—Blockhouse No. 2 Malmédy* scrawled in blood across a wall in his cell. The Nazis had taken

Nicolette deep into the Hürtgen Forest to the town of Malmédy, and Blockhouse No. 2 was the medical experimentation building.

Laurent would take the ridge, and with the extra ammunition and petrol, his forces could take the city. It was now or never. His troops would be reduced to a few beleaguered regiments if they waited any longer.

"Prepare your troops. We will take the flat at sunrise."

"But, sir—" The sergeant hesitated as he watched Laurent's expression change. Laurent stiffened and braced his emotions. Cold, calculating facts were the tools of survival, not emotions or temptations.

He thought of the mission. He was going against everything he was trained for. It was a mad compulsion, this love of his for a child and her sister. It was irrevocable, unconditional. He was sick of tolerating orders that could not defeat the enemy. The war had begun because countries tolerated atrocities instead of fighting them. It was a testament to failure; life in his country was over and only death remained. He would push on, no matter the cost.

It was Thanksgiving. Laurent, the French *Maquis*, and wounded Americans had gathered in the town's small chapel assisting the injured, wrapping them in parachutes to keep them warm. Belgian civilians who donated sides of beef and corn had prepared a feast in the chapel basement.

"This is one luxury we have in abundance," Laurent said, and then stood from the trestle table and raised his glass filled with brandy. "As for humor, I would like to share a poem with you in anticipation of the holiday season." He slipped a piece of paper from his jacket and read from it:

"Christmas will not be celebrated this year.

The Blessed Virgin and the Little Jesus are displaced persons, Saint Joseph is in a concentration camp.

The Stable has been requisitioned

The Angels have been brought down by anti-aircraft fire

The Three Kings are in England

The cow is in Berlin, and the ass in Rome

And the star has been repainted blue by order of the Chief!"

"*À votre santé*, Schnee-Eifel, *à tout prix!*" The men gave a cheer to the town they would soon encounter, then gulped down their brandy.

Christina settled quietly beside Laurent and then clutched his hand under the table.

"Do not worry. Soon, we will find Nicolette," he promised.

She nodded at a soldier wrapped in bandages. "That could be Nicolette—or you."

"You must have faith."

Christina's voice wavered somewhere between exhaustion and lunacy. "Faith is all I have left; reality is what I can't face. We are out of medical supplies. The containers of blood never landed. In addition, we search for the surgeons' gliders night and day, but they do not come. All I can do is give the men brandy and splice their bodies with pieces of tape. Even if you and Nicolette do return, there will be nothing left to mend your bones!"

It made no sense to her, a hostile battle that killed men senselessly and made their families suffer. She was tired of the endless mending of bones and bandage wrapping, of horrible wounds and the nauseating smells and endless shrieks of suffering. Perhaps it was foolish to think so much, to search for answers, she thought.

She was weary of analyzing and worrying, living life with the same dreary contempt day in and day out, each minute filled with a maelstrom of toil, fatigue, and boredom. She wondered when it would end: the thinking of Nicolette and wondering if she were alive, and wrestling with the interminable minutes of her absence, and imagining her as she left her: being brave, eyes wide with repressed tears.

"Then faith is even more essential," Laurent said. And faith was all they had, he thought—the entire lot of them. Tomorrow, they would battle Goliath with a slingshot.

Hitler's Fifth Panzer Army had the most powerful tanks in the world.

The Royal Tiger tank was 34 feet long and weighed 68 tons. It was protected by steel armor 7 inches thick and mounted a 17-foot, 88-millimeter cannon weighing 20 tons.

There would be no contest in a shoot-out with U.S.-made Sherman tanks. He also knew the Germans were well acquainted with the dense woodlands, deep valleys, and rugged ravines, and the twists and turns in vital roads that would carry their killer Panzer divisions to battle. Top American commanders were preoccupied with attacks in other areas and would be of little assistance. There was only one thing left that could turn the tide in his favor: Laurent would pray for bad weather.

He fell into his bunk and thought of the battle that would rage in just a few short hours. They were miles away, but he could hear the unmistakable screech of the screaming meemies, and the thud of the five-barreled rocket launchers pulverizing the ground, shaking what felt like the whole world.

Consumed with impatience, he threw his blanket back and sat up. The faraway booming grew louder, the air was oppressive, and he could not breathe. He walked to the door and opened it wide.

Christina stood shuddering down the hall in her doorway, her ear cocked to the sound of the bombs, trying to detect from which direction they came. "I can't sleep. I'm so frightened, I—" Laurent rushed to her and she buried her head into his chest. "Hold me," she said. He wrapped his arms around her and held her close. "You can't sleep either, can you?" she asked, examining the dark hollows around his eyes.

He stroked her long, silky hair. "I am fine."

Demolition charges hammered the ground, shaking the wooden planks beneath their feet, and flame-throwers exploded fire into the night sky, splashing eerie shadows across the room. He closed the door and pulled her into him and she locked into his embrace, her pulse pounding with the certainty of death. His lips fell to her long, slender neck.

"Unlock your heart," he begged, and suddenly she wanted him.

The demolition charges were silenced and then a hand siren wailed. The door burst open.

"I beg your pardon, sir," the captain said, then averted his eyes. "Our units have been alerted by General Bradley to move out. Aerial reconnaissance has noted vehicular traffic heading toward Schonberg. The general thinks it's routine relief of a German unit pulling out of line, but he wants it checked, just in case."

"*Ballon d'essai*," Laurent mumbled.

"Sir?"

"A trial balloon; a smoke screen! It has not occurred to the general that the Germans have the wherewithal to mount a major counteroffensive, and it'll be fought here, not in the Rhine, or the Saar, or the Roer river area, or wherever hell else the American commanders are concentrating their attacks."

"Our lines are too thinly held, sir."

General Bradley's quixotic decision, Laurent thought sarcastically. One lightly armed cavalry group, an armored division, and three infantry divisions; two of them exhausted and the other green. It was suicide.

"Why won't the general listen to you?" Christina groaned. For the first time, she truly believed the French *Maquis* would be defeated. The thought of losing Nicolette brought it all home; brought the full terror of war as nothing had before. The Germans would annihilate every soldier holding the line, and a backup would never make it in time.

"Prepare the men and check the fields for supply drops," Laurent ordered, then dismissed the captain. "I had reported my sightings: the hospital trains, the flat-cars burdened with tiger tanks, the motor traffic at night," he said, "but the intelligence experts either ignored them or misread them, thinking the Germans were moving units to Aachen or Saar, the areas threatened by American attacks."

"My divisions had clearly heard the sound of motors on their front, and there was the captured document revealing the existence of special commando units. The Fifth and Sixth Panzer Armies were withdrawn from the Northern Front, but we could not locate them on the document. They are preparing their counteroffensive right under our noses! General Bradley considered me overwrought, impetuous, and suggested I rest!"

He pulled Christina back into him. "And you," he said frantically, "my conscience battles me night and day, a tug of war between you and my soldiers."

"What do you mean?"

"I have fallen in love with you, damn it! And now I find myself risking judgment, honor, and even human lives, for your affection."

"So, this is my fault?" she asked, appalled by his accusation.

"Like my grandfather before me, I am constantly preoccupied with the material and moral situation of my soldiers, never wanting to engage them uselessly or sacrifice them. I love and respect my comrades and they, in turn, have dedicated to me their lives, absolutely. I am of the school of silence and meditation and neglect the vain appearance of the world to concentrate all my efforts on the task I have accepted."

"Now, my judgment has become clouded. I am doing things with only you in mind. I am risking the lives of my comrades, and I do not care. It is you, only you!" He spewed the words wildly, fearful there would not come another day. "My men will freeze to death without proper clothing, and it is my doing. I ordered extra petrol and ammunition in lieu of warm clothing and boots, my mind focused only on rescuing Nicolette."

Christina muffled a sob. It was all so horrible, she thought. War had made people do horrible things; even love was a horrible thing.

"Oh, I wish—I wish I were a man." She pushed from his embrace. "I'd choke you as sure as you're standing!"

"You will have to wait in line."

She ran to the door and tugged on the rusty knob, desperate to set herself free, but it fell loose into her hand.

Laurent walked toward her and she turned and took aim with it. "Don't you dare take another step, or I'll—"

"You'll what?"

"I'll—I'll throw it; so help me, I will!"

Laurent sidestepped her wild pitch and grabbed her arm, took her face, and held it while she squirmed to set herself free.

"There is no time left," he said desperately. "The earth will soon inherit our bones and yet you still cannot see! You struggle to possess something that you will never attain, and the vital impetus, the love of your life, stands before you and yet eludes you. You are only capable of erecting barriers against love, but, my sweet *âme perdue*, even the Friesians with their barriers of metal poles and razor tips couldn't halt the advancing cavalry."

She twisted and turned, wrenching her face from his large hands. She was furious at her vulnerability, and his galvanizing stare incensed her even more. He tightened his grip and pulled her back into him, his breath hot and moist against her face.

His mouth hungrily devoured hers, and she soon realized none of it mattered. They were all going to die, and she would never see Nicolette or Liam again. She slid her arms around Laurent's waist and embraced him.

His nearness was comforting, and a curious contentment swept her as he gently eased her onto the bed.

It was as if nothing else existed, as if time had ceased. His thundering heart pressed hard, unfurling a passion she had never known. Nicolette, Liam, the war, everything that mattered, faded into a pastiche of swirling fire.

"Tell me you love me."

Dreamily, she opened her eyes. His rugged face was dark against the moonlight, his smoldering eyes filling her.

"Please tell me before I go."

She struggled to say the words.

Laurent pulled her roughly to him and kissed her cruelly, as if to avenge her silence.

She choked back a cry and squirmed to set herself free. Suddenly, he released her.

"You are like this war," he said icily. "Cold and unforgiving, and I'll be damned if I know what my fascination is with the both of you! I must go. I have committed yet another injustice to my men, who wait patiently outside that door with fear knotted in their throats. I am pathetic for being taken with you, and do not look so shocked; we share the same penchant."

"You, with your eyes for your aging senator, and I, with you. But even I know a stubborn mind cannot suppress the primitive, inescapable frenzy of carnal gratification. I gave you me and you gave me you, and I know I will never find that again." He rose from the bed, stomped to the door, and heaved his shoulder into it.

Christina sat speechless, his words piercing one by one. He was right, no one would ever take the place of Liam; he would own her mind, body, and soul forever. And she didn't even know if he was alive. All her letters had still gone unanswered; at times, she had imagined the worst.

Laurent turned quickly and studied her. "My words are useless." He looked at the door lying at his feet and shrugged. "I may as well have been talking to the door." Then his demeanor changed, as if his body had entwined with hers again. He took a deep breath, then turned and walked out.

Chapter 17

The stinging cold wind began to blow from the north as the French convoy headed toward Schonberg. They traveled in the muck at a snail's pace with little sleep. Laurent stood in a field directing traffic and scanned the hell-bent, unshaven men as they fronted the quagmire. "We'll have to vacate," one of the men bellowed, then dropped from his tank. "We're sitting ducks for German artillery."

"Keep moving!" Laurent shouted and pointed toward the north. "In an hour, the wind will freeze this road solid."

Foot soldiers and tanks soon rolled into the outskirts of Saint-Vith. They established headquarters in an old hunting lodge, and sentries were stationed around the building. Inside, the men lay crumpled on the floor, too exhausted to crawl into their bedrolls. Laurent sat by candlelight and studied the terrain of the northern Hürtgen Mountains. His skill as a geographic engineer would be put to a grueling test in the next few days. He pushed himself from the table and stretched his aching back.

The patriots lay sprawled before him in a snarl of limbs, helmets, and guns. His men were from all walks of life. More than half of them were military cadets, and the rest were ordinary people: bakers, teachers, and fishermen. He scanned their young faces, envious of their coma-like sleep, and prayed for their swiftness of decision and courage in the face of death—things that made leaders, and depended on neither title nor rank.

He wished he could shield them from the horror of war, for he so loved them, these men, the French *Maquis* who thronged in by the thousands to defend their country. He was filled with anguish for what he had done, worsening their crises with insufficient provisions and materials.

Nevertheless, they had understood, for they too had shared his grief over Operation *Cri de Coeur*. They would bypass Schonberg and push on to Malmédy to continue the only operation they perceived as significant. They realized their mark on earth, and Nicolette and Operation *Cri de Coeur* was paramount.

Clumps of snow pelted from the beech trees, a thud here and a thud there sounded into the crystal cold of twilight. Laurent shivered, his lungs aching from the biting air. He folded his arms against his chest and paced between the straw-roofed bivouacs. He kicked at a tin can, once a soldier's desert stove, and as it broke apart, he could smell the gasoline used to heat the sand in it—no one took the comfort of heat for granted.

He prayed that Nicolette had survived the bitter cold. Never had he known such a sweet, brave child, and he ached at the sight of her wrapped safely in Christina's arms. Fear and the urgency of war had blinded Christina to so many things, he thought. She needed time to sort things out, and he would give her that and more: he would give her Nicolette.

The crescent moon glittered over the Belgian forest. It was beautiful, he thought, a surreal contrast to the twisted, splintered trunks protruding from the charred forest. He stopped pacing and stood: the stillness too quiet, too calm, and there came to his ears a far-off sound as if thunder approaching.

Tiny pinpoints of light began flicking along the skyline and he froze, instantly conscious of muzzle flashes from thousands of guns along the German line. As he strained to listen, the far-away firing grew louder, and from out of nowhere, a low-flying aircraft zoomed overhead. Gunfire cracked. He dove into a foxhole, his mind racing, the assault hastening his every calculation.

He peered from the hole into the sky. The stars were abundant and brilliant in the west, but above them and to the east, it was black with cumulus clouds. His eyes saw figments, silhouettes that shifted and swayed against the shadowed mountains.

Then he heard it again, and his stomach knotted: a sickening whine from the sky, then a low, deafening rumble, and through the trees, he watched in horror as the roof of the hunting lodge mushroomed into the air. Seconds later, flaming embers and bits and pieces of his men tumbled down around him, landing in grotesque positions: a molten-hot rifle, a boot, a gas mask, a helmet, and a field jacket. Death glutted his will to carry on, and he cursed helplessly. He wanted to die with them.

In a daze, he crawled from the foxhole and stumbled onto the battlefield. He heard moans and crying and praying. A dense fog had rolled from the mountains, eclipsing the moon.

He moved through the vapor in a slow-motion nightmare, tripping over them. He saw German infantrymen rooting survivors from their foxholes with flame-throwers. He dropped to the ground and rolled into a ravine. The smell of burning flesh drew near; a dull thud, an occasional shriek, a gunshot, and then silence—it repeated over and over, the minutes dragging like a wounded animal.

It was tangible now, the psychotic grip that engulfed him, the one infinite thread that distinguished man from beast. He heard orders being shouted as the Nazis walked among the men and kicked them in the groin to see if they were dead, a spray of bullets if they screamed. A stray shot here, a stray shot there, another scream. Tears squeezed from his eyes; he was cracking, losing control.

"*À corps perdu!*" he mumbled, pounding his fists into the sides of his helmet. His grandfather's words suddenly screamed at him: "Until the loss of the body, you will fight! Fight to assure justice for the glory of France and for those who have already died for it. Atone those who have suffered much. Until the loss of the body! Until the loss of the body! Until the loss of the body!" The words sounded over and over, stifling the sound of the tanks as they rolled by.

Soon, the crushing of the prostrate bodies ceased. The shooting and screams ceased. He lay broken, staring into the sky, the wind stirring the pine forest and the sunrise burning away the fog.

He would never be the same. He was beginning to see the unseeable, a thousand years in time. He saw himself and his life as a speck in the universe. He thought of his men as he had seen them last. He saw their sacrifices and his own as nothing, as a mere ripple upon the tide of France's liberation, a minuscule dent in her sovereignty.

"You all right, sir?" a voice whispered in French atop the ravine.

Laurent looked up into the fear-mired face of Jean-Baptiste Mercier, his *chef d'étatmajor*. He climbed heavily out of the ravine. "God in Heaven!" he cried and took Jean-Baptiste to him. They crawled on their bellies toward the woods. Small arms opened, but they made it safely into a thicket.

"Hell, it's good to see you!" Jean-Baptiste gave Laurent another bear hug. "Jesus Christ, I heard the bastards laughing!"

Laurent slumped and turned to look at the charred remains of the hunting lodge, and at the fire, orange against the snow, its flames whipped by a sudden wind. He stared at the columns of mist intermingling between his comrades frozen in red snow. He would return to bury them and pray for their souls, and speak of their courage and love of France. He would atone for their suffering.

"No one loved those men more than I." He spoke softly, in a trance, and their fate tore swiftly in and out of his mind. A thousand times he saw their faces hushed in death, and he knew he would wake and sleep with the vision for the rest of his life.

Perhaps his report of the slaughter would stiffen General Eisenhower's backbone. He dismissed the thought. There was a better way.

The morning mist was bathed in an eerie glow. Powerful German searchlights glanced off low-hanging clouds illuminating American positions. Laurent and Jean-

Baptiste made their way along an abandoned road littered with slabs of concrete chunks and reinforcing rods. A truck frame from an American convoy lay in a heap alongside the road, and they scoured through it collecting weather-soaked GI equipment and rations, and then dressed themselves in uniforms stripped from Nazi casualties.

Under the cover of low clouds, they sped to the end of the clearing and the beginning of the forested ravines and gorges. Along the way, they removed markings from key roads, the Germans' standard warning of minefields.

Three days later, Laurent stood atop a bluff and looked through his binoculars at the forested town of Malmédy. He spied an American supply dump next to a small landing field used by artillery observation planes.

"There are at least a hundred GIs polishing Panzer brass," Laurent said and handed his binoculars to Jean-Baptiste.

Jean-Baptiste focused on the dump. "Jesus Christ! They're fueling Peiper's SS Panzer tanks!"

Laurent slung a file of bullets around his shoulder. "Stay here until I give you a signal." He barreled up into a wooded flat that afforded him a sweeping view of Colonel Joachim Montrose's battalion of paratroop infantry. An SS sergeant stood with his machine gun aimed behind a barricade of shivering GIs. A group of twenty or so men, stripped of their clothing, were marching to the rear with their hands over their heads.

Another sergeant stepped forward, took aim with his pistol, and shot them, one by one.

Laurent plunged down the flat into a clearing and then signaled, and Jean-Baptiste rolled down beside him.

"What'd you see?" he panted.

"It's Montrose. A regiment of American prisoners are being shot, one by one—their heads blown off."

"That explains the grunt work."

"I'm going," Laurent said.

"You can't mean it! You're not going down there!"

"When the petrol tanks blow, come out shooting. Remember, do nothing until you see the tanks blow."

The naked GIs shivered in the arctic gust, praying and cursing in short, audible breaths. Iron gyres bound their ankles as they struggled to the forward line. Most were obedient, accommodating commands that were shouted, seeking only to be granted a swift end to their lives.

Laurent reached the edge of the gasoline dump. Drums containing hundreds of gallons of fuel were stacked by the road leading to the airfield. He heaved a grenade into the dump, touching off a giant conflagration of flame and smoke and knocking a handful of guards into the air.

It was credulous, much too elementary, Laurent thought. He had expected overpowering resistance. He darted in and out of the explosive chain reactions, then sped toward an artillery jeep and flung himself over the side, and drove toward the landing field. It was vacant except for a group of American prisoners sprawled on the ground, shielding their heads against a blast.

"Give 'em hell!" shouted a GI as Laurent screeched to a halt. The GI clambered up into the jeep and raised the antitank gun toward the line of Germans racing toward them.

His hands gripped the trigger, the muzzle flashed, and the missile screamed through the air.

"Strike!" the GI whooped, and Laurent sped toward the SS Panzer tank unit stationed next to the hangar. A round of bullets from a burp gun hit the GI and burst his chest open. He slumped over the gun, and the missile shot toward the Germans.

"Hit!" Laurent yelled, his adrenaline soaring and numbing the bullet hole in his thigh. He thrust his thumb into the gaping fissure. It was a clean in-and-out wound. "*Bêtise!*" he screamed in anger.

He slid his belt from his trousers and bound it around his leg above the wound to stop the flow of blood. Desperately, he looked about him. A Nazi infantryman came from behind and aimed his flame-thrower. The flare burst and Laurent fell out of the jeep and writhed helplessly on the ground, his cry a crazed gargle.

**

A grin crinkled the corners of Colonel Joachim Montrose's beady eyes as he peered down at his captive. "Sixth SS Panzer Division welcomes you to Malmédy," he announced coldly.

Laurent lay frozen in pain, his heartbeat slamming in his ears. The fire inside spread like snake venom through each extremity of his body, and the odor of burned flesh churned his nostrils. "You are pork for the *charcuterie!*" Colonel Montrose shouted as he ran his finger along his large, silver knife with its short straight-edged blade. "I will deliver your head personally to the duchess."

He laughed cruelly. "I want you to die not knowing what my plans are for your precious Nicolette. I am only sorry that I did not find Christina first, but my quest is still young. Yes, at long last, my time has come! My wife will be horrified, but once again, I will master her, and she will have her rightful place at my side and live an ordered life!"

He felt complete, masterful, and blood ran hot through his veins as he eyed the gleaming edge of the *parang* and slashed it through the air ritualistically—one, two, three times. "Heil Hitler!" he cried like a triumphant rooster.

Laurent opened his mouth and groaned. He could feel each breath sputter in his lungs. He turned his head and looked across the camp at the gasoline fires. In his memory, he saw Christina and Nicolette reflected in the raging inferno, and he studied them, memorizing the features of their faces, their bright onyx eyes, the color of their lips, and wind-swept hair. He groaned again, but faintly this time, a hoarse, wistful sound, and he felt the wings of flight begin to take him from the pain.

"I love you, my sweet," he heard Christina's voice. "Come to me." The warm fragrance of her skin breathed into him. "*Tout de suite*," he mumbled incoherently. He watched the *parang* run slowly, deliberately, the length of his body, and he wrenched his wrists against the rope constraints until they bled, and the rage that found no words and the tenacity that knew no bounds suddenly died within him. It was of no use, he thought; death would be sweet, and he squeezed his eyes shut and braced himself.

Colonel Montrose rose to his full height, tightened his grip, and sliced the blade downward.

The shot was thunderous as it tore through the Colonel's hand and the *parang* then spiraled them through the air. They dropped at the feet of the SS guards and, in a split second, their bodies were riddled with gaping holes. The Colonel's legs buckled, and he came toppling forward, scarlet mist squirting from his stump onto Laurent like a pulsating fountainhead.

A voice cursed out loud: *"Blitzkrieg!* You bastard krauts!"

Laurent squeezed his eyes and rode the swell of pain. He heard the shuffle of feet, the slice of the knife that released his constraints, the victory cheers of GIs, and then he heard a voice cry out, "Jean-Baptiste!" and realized it was his own.

Chapter 18

Colonel Montrose watched helplessly as the bridge spanning the main river into Malmédy was blown up in his face. His Panzer division would be delayed for weeks.

"I should kill him!" Jean-Baptiste said, squinting through his gunsight and riding it down the Colonel's body. The gun stilled at his crotch. "*Adieu!*"

"Not yet, my comrade," Laurent said and pushed the muzzle aside.

Jean-Baptiste swung the gun down to the Colonel's crotch again and his eye remained focused.

"Damn it! You know he's our guarantee in the camp!" Laurent shouted.

Reluctantly, Jean-Baptiste put the gun down and lit a cigarette. He drew hard, then puckered his mouth and blew a smoke ring on the Colonel's face. "He's mine when we've taken the camp."

Laurent ignored him, lost in thought. Slowly, the mournful sounds increased until they filled him, echoing in his mind, the dead, the half-dead, their cries, and their prayers. Rage began to churn again, and he tried to suppress it. He had to. Colonel Montrose would be of no use to him dead.

He stared into the fire. He thought of Christina, Nicolette, his constant preoccupation emotionally using him up. He would never be the same; his love for them had changed all that. He saw Christina beside him on the bed, her face, her eyes, how he had left, and the emptiness he had felt.

He watched a plume of smoke rise from the remains of the Malmédy bridge. A lone sparrow fell to earth, its singed wings flapping spasmodically in the snow. He thought of the *kinderkamp*, a fortress of steel stocked with enough food, ammunition, and fuel to last through several sieges. He knew it would be an impractical feat for his handful of bravos—more like suicide. Yes, the Colonel was his only hope.

"You have the expression of a ticking bomb. What is it?" Jean-Baptiste asked.

"Tomorrow we storm the camp, *l'improviste*."

"The Colonel?"

"Keep him in your pocket." Laurent wiped his brow.

**

It was dawn by the time Christina slipped into the portal of the Saint-Etienne Ribbon Factory. She handed a passer to the man at the door, who whisked her down the stairs and into the basement.

"Wrap her in blankets," the guard said to a small, brown-skinned woman. "Feed her some soup."

Christina nodded gratefully.

"Poor thing is nearly frozen," the woman said to the boy at her side. "Light a fire under the pot."

The young boy tugged at his ear, and Christina looked at him questioningly.

"A fire," the woman enunciated and waved the boy across the room. "Nazis clubbed him and left him for dead," she explained.

Christina's eyes followed the boy as he lit the fire. "I'm going to claw out the beating heart of those monsters!" she snarled. "God as my witness!"

The old woman met her eye; they were both thinking it: Revenge would be gratifying. "Reminds me of a joke I heard from a prisoner at the *Vélodrome d'Hiver*," the old woman said.

"Did you know at 9:20 last night, a Jew killed a Nazi soldier at Luxembourg, then cut his heart out and ate it?"

"No," Christina said.

"Like I said, it was a joke. The Nazi has no heart, Jews don't eat pork, and at 9:20 everybody is listening to the BBC!"

It had been a long while since Christina had had such a gratifying chuckle, and she admired the woman, for she had not forgotten how to laugh. "Last evening, I listened to Radio Berlin hoping to hear of a turn in the war. Something, anything, to calm my fears about my little sister, Nicolette. She's in Malmédy in Blockhouse No. 2."

"Malmédy?" The old woman looked stricken.

"Yes, Hitler's *kinderkamp*."

"Are you going alone?" the old woman choked.

"Yes, I figure I'll have plenty of cover during nightfall."

"You must not go, you'll be killed! An army of men could not penetrate it. That camp is the German *Meisterwerk!*"

"It doesn't matter!" Christina spoke abruptly. "I don't care if I die! Life isn't worth living without her!" It was always her anxiety and fear running rampant. She felt it every waking moment, which was why she had left Bastogne. It was unthinkable for her to stay behind and let things slide and hope for the best. She watched the boy struggle to light the fire and then looked at the old woman. "Surely, you must understand!" she declared.

The old woman followed Christina's eyes and nodded. Yes, she understood, and it would be futile to dissuade the young girl. "I have a map of the *kinderkamp* you seek. We also have a German vehicle. Rasha will drive you as far as safety permits. It is best that you travel by moonlight. There are three more evenings of good light. If you leave tomorrow, you should have plenty of time."

The old woman wrapped a blanket snugly around Christina and looked at her sweet face. It was a curious thing, she thought, how everything reduced itself to animal instinct.

She had seen it countless times: the primeval fear, especially in women and children.

Perhaps it would be the young girl's salvation.

The jeep pulled out of the machine shed and stopped at the portal. The old woman ushered Christina into the vehicle and placed a bundle beside her.

"Shalom aleichem," she smiled a toothless grin, then slunk out of sight.

"Micha wishes you well," Rasha said. "We should arrive at our first safe house before dawn."

The frozen shore of the Furan River was a graveyard of abandoned tanks. Everywhere Christina looked, there was desolation and ruin. Piles of scorched and twisted metal from demolished iron foundries and tumbled masonry from ribbon factories littered the roadside. She looked at Rasha. Deep lines of fatigue were etched on his large, round face and around his blue eyes. Bright red hair poked out in ringlets from under his stocking cap.

"You're very kind," she said.

"Think nothing of it. I've done this dozens of times. Perhaps you'll be the lucky one."

"How many have there been?" she asked grimly.

"I am saddened to tell you how many, but I also understand, the soul will not let go of hope."

Christina suddenly felt like a minuscule seed in a pasture of thistles. They were silent as they bumped along the rutted road in the old jeep and after a while, intrigued by his dialect, she spoke. "Where are you from?"

"Russia. I am a Russian Jew."

"How did you meet Micha?"

"I escaped from a concentration camp. Dachau. She lived in the countryside and took me in."

"What was it like in Dachau?"

"They gave me pliers to pull the gold teeth from the corpses. Ja, it was my job."

The spasm began in Christina's throat, and the sick liquid rose into her mouth, and she swallowed it, willing it away until she could speak again. Rasha's voice was a monotone, she thought, detached from life, but nothing surprised her anymore. How much could one take?

"How did you escape?"

There was a long silence, as if he were fearful of breaking. "I informed on other Jews," he said remorsefully.

"And I robbed them to get in with the SS. They gave me food and assurances that I would be set free."

His expression was worse than she had seen in a hunted animal. He began to babble in Russian, and she turned from him, struggling to gather her wits.

Rasha muttered a psalm, and it seemed to calm him. He could not help himself, she reasoned. The Germans had stolen his morality and forced him to do things only a madman was capable of. A flicker lit the horizon, and Christina strained her eyes in the direction of the mountains. It flickered again, and then an orange ball of fire shot into the air.

"What is that?" She asked.

Rasha laughed. "The pyres. They are burning the corpses." He laughed again, only louder and longer, a deep belly laugh. Soon, tears filled his eyes and rolled in streaks down his big red cheeks.

"Why are you laughing?" Christina asked, aghast.

"The SS—" He doubled over. "Dumb sons of bitches haven't discovered a way to extinguish the fire from the ash heaps. They're worried—" He wiped his tears with the back of his hand. "—worried the fires will give away their positions to Allied air."

For a pathetic instant, Christina felt like laughing with him, but the thought of the heaps of human bones burning night and day in the ashen pits made her sick. War had taken Rasha's mind, transformed him into a babbling lunatic, and she was not far behind.

Rasha took a handkerchief from his coat pocket and blew his nose, then looked at Christina and shrugged embarrassingly. "Please tell me of America."

At the mention of America, Christina sat for a few moments and tried to compose herself.

"It is beautiful, is it not?" Rasha's eyes sparkled.

"Yes," she said and then smiled thoughtfully. "It is the most beautiful place in the world." She believed her father's words: "It is a free country, a safe country. A good place to raise a family where a hard, honest day of work pays off."

She wished she had taken the time to listen to father, to understand and be like him. She had lost his world the moment she took for granted all of his glorious dreams. Father worked the earth and lived in poverty, and it should have been enough, but it had been beneath her dignity to indulge in such a life. She had chosen instead to coerce a miracle.

All her life, she had heard sneers and jokes slung at them, and now she realized that ridicule was based only on pompousness. No amount of poverty could have made father feel ashamed because he was of good stock, and beliefs, blended with a good attitude, the kind of things few people in the world possess.

Rasha flung his arm protectively against Christina and slammed on the brakes and then pulled over to the edge of the road.

"What is it?" Christina jolted forward.

"Something's in the road." He swung out of the jeep and ran toward the shadowy heap. "It's a body, a Nazi!"

Christina leaped out and ran toward Rasha. The body was weather-soaked and bloated, and the face, as near as Christina could tell, was that of a young boy.

"We should bury him," she said despondently.

"No!" Rasha commanded.

"Where I come from, we bury the children!" she shouted.

"He's a member of the 12th SS Panzer Hitler Youth Division. Look at his armband!" Rasha pointed. "It's an élite unit with a reputation for ignoring accepted rules of war. They have committed heinous crimes!"

Angrily, he kicked the bloody glove from his path. Christina shrieked when she saw the boy's small hand still inside of it.

"We will bury him!" she commanded.

Rasha's shimmering eyes concentrated on Christina. "I will not do it! While fighting on the Eastern Front, these boys executed four thousand of my fellow prisoners in reprisal for killing six captured SS by Russian secret police! You will have to bury him yourself! I am leaving!"

Christina's hair blew wildly about her like glossy black ribbons. She pulled it from her face and slung her rifle to the ground. "Like you left your fellow men in Dachau?"

Rasha focused on the young boy. His big shoulders slumped and he fell to his knees and began to sob.

Christina wished desperately she had not scolded him. She looked at the boy's unseeing eyes. But he was just a child, and a child didn't deserve to die, no matter where he came from. She picked up her rifle and walked to a small bomb crater in the field. The earth was soft inside, pulverized by an impact. She sat beside it and sifted the fine black soil between her fingers and watched it swirl away in the wind.

Again, her fears for Nicolette assaulted her, rushing, here and there like crows circling over sprouting corn. She willed herself not to think; there was not the time. She stood, then dug in with the butt of her rifle, and shoveled out the loose dirt.

After a time, she lay weak-kneed in the hollow and stared up at the dawn. It began to snow, and she felt the crystals brush her face, softly tickling like the silky down clusters from the acacia trees back home. She saw Nicolette's crooked little grin, her small fists clenched at her side, and her feet dancing with excitement as she galloped into her arms.

Surely, tomorrow or the next day, she would find her, and surely, she would be all right. Christina took a moment and said a prayer.

Rasha stood over her. "I will finish," he said softly and lifted the corpse and laid it into the crater. His large hands scooped dirt over the young boy and carefully patted it smoothly.

He stood, then dropped his gaze before Christina and shrugged helplessly.

"We both know war is wrong," Christina said tenderly. She wanted to speak soothing words, to comfort Rasha, to collapse into his arms and cry with him, but she knew the gesture would break them both.

It was two days before they reached the outskirts of Malmédy. They stood on a bluff and scanned the rolling valleys and lower slopes of the Vosges Mountains with their binoculars.

"Too foggy," Rasha complained.

"It'll be a good cover."

"I need a visual layout before we proceed," he insisted.

"We could be stuck here for days. I say we go!" Christina pulled two blankets from the jeep and gouged a hole with her pocketknife into the middle of each. "Put this on. It'll be a good camouflage."

"It's a chamber of horrors," Rasha said, scanning the edge of the Hürtgen Forest.

"You'll not dissuade me," she said firmly and tossed a blanket at his feet.

"If the Germans and the weather don't finish us, the terrain will!" He picked up the blanket and tossed it into the jeep. "Down there is a belt of rolling woodland twenty miles long with fir trees measuring one hundred feet tall—perfect for tree bursts."

Christina dropped to her knees. "Then this is where we part. Goodbye, Rasha." She slid down the embankment, and then crawled through the forest, her eyes and hands carefully appraising the woodland path for mine wires. She spotted an armored column from a German division about a kilometer ahead of her, and she heard Rasha's voice call out, "The ravine, beside you, run for it!" She eyed it and ran to its edge, then rolled down into a river of icy water. Rasha sped through the path and rolled down behind her.

"Stand up, keep moving!" he shouted. "You'll freeze to death!"

He lifted her from the river like a drowned kitten and laid her on the ground, then began pumping her arms and legs. "One, two, three, pump! One, two, three, pump! You must keep moving!" He quickly stripped her clothes and wrapped her in his bedroll, then heated pebbles in a can and poured them into her shoes and onto her clothing.

"You risked your life." Christina's teeth chattered. And until that moment, she hadn't realized how much she needed Rasha.

"Brave men lived before Agamemnon." He smiled. "We must hurry. The German division is heading toward the Rhine, north of the forest. We will follow them. They'll lead us to the *kinderkamp* and," he grinned, "they will clear the minefields for us."

On Christmas Day, they entered Malmédy, inching their way through rubble-filled alleys. The cold air hung with the smell of broken gas mains, sewage, and dead animals. The Germans were rooting American troops out of storm sewers with grenades and flame-throwers.

Christina rested against a beam in an abandoned cellar. "The meek shall inherit the earth," she muttered, still out of breath. She examined the devastation surrounding them. "If women took charge, we wouldn't be in such a mess and there would never be war! Think about it, Rasha. We are the healers, the teachers, the caregivers, and the negotiators. Women have never instigated war or inhumane cruelty. Female animals will not abandon their young, but males will kill them."

Rasha nodded, smiling and noncommittal, and then sat beside her and pulled her boots off. He shook the wet straw out and refilled them with dry straw. They heard the Nazis marched in columns along the streets, and dust fell from the rafters. "Damned doryphores!" he mumbled.

"What's a doryphore?" Christina asked.

"It's a damned green-backed potato beetle. Worst plague a farmer can face and a particularly galling name to be called."

"I can think of some myself," Christina muttered with disgust.

"A few more kilometers, and with some luck, you will see your little sister. You are up to it, *ja*?" He took her frozen feet into his large hands and rubbed them hard.

It had been so long, Christina thought that she had almost forgotten what Nicolette looked like, and she felt all the desolate feelings swarm over her, feelings so many others surely felt. She looked at Rasha. He slid her foot deep into the cushion of the straw, and suddenly she felt comforted. "What keeps you going, Rasha?"

He pulled a wooden box next to her and sat down and rested his face in his rag swathed hands. "The will to live is powerful," he said, sighing heavily. "I have witnessed the murder of my family, the fear of facing death square in the eye, the gnawing hunger, endless bitter cold, so cold it could snap a bone in two."

"And you still wish to live?"

"Life is only a fleeting liaison for the wandering soul, but lately, I've come to grasp its truth: the feelings of another person's misery, the faraway look in a dead child's eyes, man's inhumanity to man, rage, helplessness. These past few days have afforded me a chance to clear my mind and harden my resolve."

"I refuse to believe my people have died without significance or worth. I cannot shut out the overwhelming facts of it all, that a small country such as Germany can hold its own against an enormous coalition. I've not lost hope that this war will somehow turn around, and if I can do something to help, it'll give me the will to survive."

He withdrew a potato from his pack. "Enough of this chatter; we must eat." He broke the vegetable in half and placed it on a wooden cable spool. He swept his arm elegantly toward it. "For you, my little *soldati.*"

The sweet gesture went to Christina's heart. She couldn't remember the last time she had eaten a potato. "It's so good," she said, smacking her lips and savoring each little bite. "Where did you come by it?"

"Chernozem," he nodded affectionately. "The black soil of Southern Russia. My grandmother mixed beetroot with it to make borsch when I was a lad."

A grenade suddenly shook the little cellar. Dust and debris rained onto them and their dinner bounced from the spool. Christina picked their potatoes up and brushed them off.

"Nothing is going to ruin my dinner," she said stoically, batting her black lashes and flicking the plaster from the table onto the floor. "I have cooked and slaved over a hot stove all day, and neither bombs nor blood nor blight will keep me from eating this fine Christmas meal!"

"It is good to find humor in this war," Rasha said with a laugh. "We have grown to be brave."

"Brave?" Christina contemplated. "I am not brave; I just don't give a hog's whisker anymore. Those Nazis are giving a new meaning to the word hate, and there is only one reason I will not run from this room and claw their faces off. For me, it is not about being brave. I would give my life gladly to find Nicolette."

Rasha gave her a conciliatory nod, and through the dim, chalky grit, he studied Christina. "You have not seen the worst," he assured her, "but you have pushed the door open a little, pushed it farther than anyone else has, and I admire that, along with your courage and iron will. *Ja*, perhaps miracles do exist. The important thing is that you keep love in your heart. Strife separates man from principle, but love mixes them together again."

Christina smiled politely and thought of Laurent and wished that she could have warmed her heart toward him. She could see him clearly now: a man in love, willing to give his life for Nicolette. How could she have been so stubborn?

Why did she not see, she asked herself again and again. Why did she always muddle simple things? "You are what I want," he had said tenderly, his strong arms locked around her, "and soon we will find Nicolette, and then we will celebrate Christmas."

It was Christmas, and Christina prayed that God was watching over them.

Chapter 19

"Excellent specimen," the German physician said, studying Nicolette's fair complexion. "She will integrate into the American masses well for a while," he calculated.

The interns tightened around the operating table, their eyes steadfast on a blue line etched across her skull.

"Our scientists have developed a serum, a highly contagious biological agent. It is extremely effective, retroactive immediately in producing abnormalities in certain areas of the brain."

The physician circled a marker around the frontal and temporal lobe. "The particular behavioral characteristics of the microorganisms depend on which area of the brain is most affected by the process. The symptoms are progressive, but the rate of degeneration varies from person to person. In this area," he slashed an 'X' with his marker, "dementia, and this," he slashed another mark, "paralysis, tremor, or impaired coordination, and so on."

He gave a long, hard look at the gathering. "We shall concentrate our efforts on dementia."

He handed a syringe to the nurse, and she attached a needle to the barrel and then filled it with a vial of gray liquid.

The physician continued his allocution. "A single injection into the bloodstream will be enough to spread the organic disorder to anyone she comes in contact with. The general population will experience a decrease in mental ability, particularly memory, and judgment. This, gentlemen, will be the decisive factor in our war: the *Führerprinzip.* It will take our enemies years to research a defense against this weapon. By then, it will be too late; the United States will be a country permeating with *dummkopfs!"*

Nicolette lay silent on the gurney, unable to comprehend the German verbiage babbling around her. She was emaciated from lack of nourishment, too weak and exhausted to speak, but had attempted with great effort to call out for the old guard who had shot the terrible man in the camp, then had brought her here where doctors would make her well.

She turned her head weakly and focused on the door. He was out there, waiting with a teacup of sugar lumps. He had promised, and she still dauntlessly believed, but she did not see the cold, calculating plan that the doctors held for her.

**

Laurent fingered a detonator in his SS uniform pocket and pointed it at Colonel Montrose as he followed him into the sprawling research headquarters. He produced identification papers for the guards and they waved him through. The impenetrable stronghold had turned out to be, much to his incredulity, a sieve: a colossal medical experimentation center, too large and haphazard for proper supervision.

From his pocket, Laurent shoved the detonator low into the Colonel's back and walked past another regiment of guards. German retaliation would be brutal, he thought. He stared ahead, rocklike, toward the double steel doors. Colonel Montrose had confessed that Nicolette was through those doors, and the thought sickened Laurent.

He wanted to kill Montrose, slowly, inch by inch, and watch him suffer. He wanted the Parisians, the *Maquis*, and the Americans to watch while he tortured him beyond the boundaries of human tolerance and ride him down without pity like he had done those who got in his way. His finger hovered over the detonator. It would be easy, he thought.

They passed a group of German interns, and Colonel Montrose nodded. Laurent shoved the detonator solid into his back, and he glared at his fat orb of a head. Master race in the raw, Laurent laughed to himself, outwitted by the French *Maquis* who were driven underground, hidden beneath the surface while he went about his killing business. He wanted to kill Montrose a thousand times over.

A nurse lifted Nicolette's bony arm and inspected it for a vein close to the skin. The overhead light flickered and the generators began to sputter. She cursed and let Nicolette's arm fall to the table.

The physician seized the nurse by the shoulders. "You must continue," he demanded. "Inject it; the electricity may be out for hours!"

Jean-Baptiste backed into the steel doors, released his pack, and pressed the detonator. In an instant, the steel doors blew inward, the flash of it lighting the room and filling it with concrete and dust. Jean-Baptiste shoved Colonel Montrose ahead of him, aimed his machine gun, and scattered the room with bullets.

Laurent searched wildly through the half-light and chalky grit. Dropping his gun, he ran toward the gurney and lifted Nicolette from it. He quickly unfastened her gown and felt the little heart he feared had stopped beating. "She is alive!" he cried.

"The truck is waiting. We must hurry." Jean-Baptiste signaled with a wave of his hand.

Laurent placed Nicolette over his shoulder, grabbed his gun, and quickly edged toward the door. He heard something and leaned against the wall. It was the clatter of boots racing, squealing around corners.

The commandant barked an order: *"Achtung!"* and the boots skidded to a halt.

Again, there was silence, and then the synchronized click of guns.

"Schlaraffenland!" the commandant shouted down the hall.

"Fool's paradise, my ass," Laurent mumbled. "Jean-Baptiste, bring the cistern over here!"

Jean-Baptiste thrust his shoulder into the cistern and jostled it toward Laurent.

Laurent mounted himself and placed Nicolette inside, then waved Jean-Baptiste after him. "Damn it! Get down here!" he whispered angrily, dismissing Jean-Baptiste's look of disbelief. "And on the way down, pitch your gun and boot through the window. That is an order!"

Jean-Baptiste threw his gun out the window and removed his boot, cursing and fumbling until he finally slipped it off and threw it out. Laurent pulled him down onto the cistern and into a pile of human hair.

"Blitzkrieg!" the commandant ordered, then stormed the room and thrust through bodies lying prostrate on the floor. "Colonel Montrose!" he screamed in horror. Colonel Montrose lay sprawled in a pool of blood separated from his legs at the hips. Orders were shouted and feet shuffled toward the broken window. *"Schweinhund! Das Ende vom Lied!"* the commandant cried.

Laurent smiled, aware that the commandant had seen Jean-Baptiste's gun and boot. In an instant, the clatter of footsteps rushed from the room. Jean-Baptiste shuddered and laughed nervously, then crawled out of the cistern. He was covered with hair. Smooth, strong tresses from young children:

Gold, platinum, and ash forming a flaxen blanket over him. He held a clump against his nose, and it smelled pure and sweet, as if just cleansed. He was unable to speak, exerting all of his willpower not to weep. The Nazis' skill in slaughter was now sinking in; the cessation of civilization was nearing an end. Laurent handed Nicolette to him, then swung out of the cistern. He saw it all in Jean-Baptiste's face; he knew his pain.

"We all fear the genocide, my comrade," Laurent said sympathetically. "But most of all, we must fear the *Kriegspiel,* the war game itself. The Allies are players of chess, seeing only one side of the board, ignorant of their opponent's moves. They have not trusted the instincts of the French *Maquis*, and it has become a misfeasance, their course of action pursued for want of anything better."

Jean-Baptiste held Nicolette tightly, and his tears fell softly, trickling down onto her face. "We are only weakened by lack of food and sleep," he said, dismissing the terrible truth.

Laurent studied Nicolette, her face all bones, eyes, and rotting teeth, and then he gently kissed her. She cracked open her eyes; they were bright with pain, and her vision hung on a ray of sunlight. She followed it until her eyes set on Laurent and a smile flickered. "My fairy angel," she whispered hoarsely, and then her eyes went to Jean-Baptiste. "Two, I have two."

Her voice pierced Laurent like a flame-thrower. Never would he lose sight of her again. "You are a dour lot, little one," he comforted and smoothed her matted curls.

"You are safe now. We will hide in the countryside, and soon you will see your sister."

**

Christina jolted awake to ear-shattering bombardments.

The battle for Hürtgen Forest had intensified, constantly demanding more and more Allied troops. A regiment of the First Division had taken a beating in the northern fringe of the forest. The Fourth Division suffered heavy losses and was sent to the Ardennes front for repairs. American commanders had been riveted into making endless sacrifices.

Unit after unit, green troops and veterans alike moved through the killing ground in a kind of perpetual nightmare.

"Fog, thick as pea soup," Rasha said, peering out of the basement window. "Once again, luck is on our side!"

Christina tore strips from the curtains and Rasha wound them tightly around her hands. "I can't let them freeze; I've much to do today," she said, and her thoughts roused with hope.

"Pad your coat with the extra curtains, and fill your boots with fresh straw," Rasha said. He took the bundle that Micha had put in the jeep and unwrapped a nurse's uniform and identification papers. "You will meet the graveyard shift at the southernmost entrance of the *kinderkamp*. In the darkness, surrounded by nurses, you will go unnoticed. From then on, you are on your own, except for this."

He reached into his pocket and withdrew a tiny pill. He scrutinized it, rolling it between his fingers, wondering about the infinitesimal numbers he had given away. His mind called up the faces, young and old alike, who had died with the same dream in their hearts. "It is made from the foxglove plant, and it will stop a heart in sixty seconds," he said. "If you are caught, take it, for death will be slow and agonizing without it."

Christina stared aghast at the prospect of her death, and she let her mind run unhurriedly over the plan again. This was no time to let her bones turn to jelly. "I had a dream last night." She swallowed, stifling the dread.

"The world exploded in all directions, and then there was nothing but darkness, the way it must've been at the beginning of time. Millions of years passed, then the pieces clumped together again and formed a new world. Then, after a time, it happened again: the explosion of the bomb, then the new creation, and so on, as if God forgave man's stupidity time and again to preserve his beloved conception."

Rasha nodded, wise with age. "Perhaps the fault lies with us for being compliant, not making our voices heard, and marching meekly to the orders of destruction. Fear is an awful thing, and bravery is rare."

The scheme of life was becoming clear, Christina thought. It was all so simple, and nothing was simpler than conviction; to fight for a cause until death snatched you.

"Death will be the only thing that will stop me," she said bravely.

"I admire your pluck." Rasha gave her a pat on the back. "I have helped many come and go, but never have I seen such determination, not even in the men is there such impervious confidence." He placed the pill into her shirt pocket.

"We must find a safe location near the camp so you can monitor activity before you make your move. I will not be waiting for you once you have left; you will have to make your own way back to the safe house. There is a Turkish tobacco freighter docked off the Ivory Coast, and the captain takes on stowaways in exchange for gold. If you and your sister survive, I will assure passage to the American consulate."

Christina watched as Rasha fussed about his pack. In him, she had found a hero. He had found his place in the war, and it had given meaning to his life. His wise Russian eyes saw clearly the truths and falsehoods in faces, and he trusted his conscience to do right by them. There were many before her and many after her whom he would risk his life for.

The nurses huddled at the southernmost entrance to the *kinderkamp*, swishing and patting their limbs for warmth.

Christina trailed behind, her face hooded by a woolen cape. Her mind began to race, recalling all Rasha'a instructions. An iron gate opened, and a bright light swept the shivering crowd. Uniformed men brandished clubs and snarled at them to form lines. The crushing maze caught Christina and pushed her forward into the blinding spotlight.

"*Handbuch, Fräulein!*" a guard ordered.

Christina went cold, her hand at her throat.

"*Handbuch!*" he growled again, this time lifting her chin with his club.

She reached into her pocket, withdrew her passport, and handed it to him. The guard flicked his eyes from it to her face two, three, four times. Abruptly, he turned.

"*Gesamtkunstwerk!*" A work of art, he shouted to a guard across the way.

The guard lumbered over and stared at Christina's pale, shivering face. "*Liebchen!*" Sweetheart! He grinned maliciously and took her by the arm through the gate and into the bastion. A silver-headed SS officer summoned them into a private chamber and ordered Christina to stand before a long table surrounded by other officers.

The guard puffed out his chest and eyed her up and down. "*Ja! Weltlust!*" Yes, luscious! He crowed like a triumphant cock, and she stood, immobilized by the cold expressions on the officers as they nodded in agreement.

The silver-headed officer made his decision with a flick of his hand, then slapped the guard on the back and offered him a cigar. She was beautiful, they had decided.

She would be sent to Dachau for Dr. Sigmund Rascher's experiments.

"Heil Hitler!" The guard raised his right hand in salutation, clicked his heels, and then swiftly led Christina to the blockhouse. He shoved her into the room, slammed the door, and tightened the bolts. Moonlight streamed in from a small window, and Christina felt her way between rows of cots. Young children with assorted ailments lay upon them, some crying mournful sounds.

She took her scarf off, held it tightly against her face to quell the stench, and then examined the gaunt faces before her, one by one, and row by row. Numbly, she felt her way through the maze, picking, poking, and turning them in hopes of finding Nicolette.

A small, quavering voice called out from across the room. "Mother—mother!"

Christina searched until she came upon the sound. "Mother—mother!" the sad-eyed girl cried again with her small, bony arms outstretched.

"She thinks you're her mother," a voice chatted offhandedly in the dark. "Pick her up, hold her, or she'll start screaming again."

Christina quickly picked up the tiny raven-haired girl and rocked her in her arms.

"We're all going to die, you know," the voice said flatly.

Christina looked in the direction of the voice. The dark, sunken eyes were unblinking, set wide under thick eyebrows, and the sharp, angular features of the girl's face exaggerated her round, bald head.

"Only if you will it," Christina said, unfazed.

"Surely you are joking," the girl ridiculed, and then muttered something in Hebrew.

"I haven't given up. You'd do well to do the same."

"You know nothing! You're the lucky one, indeed—a nurse!"

"I'm not a nurse," Christina countered. "It's only a disguise. I'm here to find my sister, Nicolette Cross. She's in Blockhouse No. 2. Perhaps, you've seen her."

"There are hundreds that come and go in here," the girl said suspiciously. "Besides, I don't believe you! You're a spy, nothing but a rotten Gestapo spy!"

"No, you must believe me!"

"No one has ever been able to break out, much less in, and live to tell about it. I say you're a rotten spy!" She spat at Christina and then took the child from her.

"No! No! They are coming for me soon. Dachau! They're taking me to a place called Dachau!"

"Well, June bugs in December," the girl taunted, "the warming experiments. I heard the nurses talking about them."

"Warming experiments?"

"Yeah, they want to find out how long it'll take a frozen man to thaw. They're using body heat from women to speed up the process. The more attractive the girl, the faster the thaw."

The sight coursed through Christina's imagination, and she would have laughed aloud had it not been for the pathetic truth. "Why?" she asked incredulously.

"Something about the temperature a pilot faces at high altitudes. The Nazis are experimenting to see how much they can stand before they die, and then the best means of rewarming them. The test persons are laid naked on a stretcher, covered with a sheet, and put outside overnight.

Every hour on the hour, water is poured over the sheet until a foot of ice covers them.”

The vision of it battered Christina. She stood and wrung her hands. “And the women?”

“As far as I know, the pretty ones are stripped and put in bed with the test person.”

“It’s insane!”

“Insane or not, it’s the truth!” The girl placed the sleeping child back into Christina’s arms. “I’ve prayed night and day to be selected for the project.”

“What?” Christina asked in horror.

“Better there than here,” she said with a shrug. “I’ve heard they give you warm food and a soft bed with sheets and blankets.”

Christina sadly surveyed the room, thinking about it. “So, it has come to this.”

“Every last one of these girls would give their souls to be chosen.”

No, Christina thought. This is not happening! It is not happening! “We’ll escape,” she said abruptly.

“Escape?” The girl howled. “This dungeon of skeletons? Why, you’re a crazed lunatic!” Her deadened eyes penetrated Christina.

“You’re all going to die anyway, you said it yourself!”

“Believe me; death will be much easier in here than in some torture chamber. We know our fate, we’re prepared, and we’ll go peacefully.”

Christina could feel the heat beneath her cheeks. The girl had systematically accepted death, and her indifference regarding the matter infuriated her. She scanned the room.

They were all like her, every last one of them, empty of life and spirit.

"Nothing matters anymore," the girl deadpanned.

"I understand, given what has happened, that you think your future no longer matters, but there is an answer."

"What's that?"

Christina saw a lifting of the girl's spirit. There was indeed a chance, a chance for all of them if she could shovel down deep enough and unearth the faith they were born with. She thought of her father. Survival had burned in his breast: Do, or die. Like Father, she would shovel and plant a seed, a seed that would grow roots and limbs and fruit.

"It's in the doing." Christina grinned. "What's your name?"

"Sondra."

"Do you like to play games, Sondra?"

"Of course!"

"Crambo?"

"Yeah."

"Then we will play!" Christina placed the little girl on the cot and then rolled up her sleeves.

"I want to be first." Sondra giggled self-consciously at the thought of her eagerness to play a child's game. "The flowers in May—" she began, then looked about the room, and pointed at a boy huddled in the corner.

He smiled a toothless grin. "Will bring another day," he said and eyed the little girl next to him.

"And my pa, if I pray," the little girl sniffed and tapped the boy in front of her.

"And my ma, If I say—" the boy smiled at Christina, and she scanned the room full of ragamuffins. They were taking notice: sitting up and rubbing red-rimmed eyes, smiles replacing sorrow.

"Faith! Faith! Have faith today!" Christina cheered them on.

"Hope! Hope! Have hope today!" a voice hollered from the far side of the room.

"Strength! Strength! Have strength today!" someone else called out.

"Fight! Fight! Fight today," a boy shouted and circled his fist in the air.

"We'll win! Win! Win today! We'll win! Win! Win today!" Christina chanted and clapped her hands to the cadence of voices fusing hers. Hope, faith, and desire drove them into a frenzy that no guard could break. They were coming together; it was in their eyes, an awakening of life, and the vigor to live it. It was time to act upon the fervor, Christina thought confidently. It was now or never.

"You!" Christina pointed to a tall, wiry boy clapping his hands above the circle of children. "Your arms are long and strong; you'll be perfect!" She nodded at another candidate. "The same goes for you! And you, and you, and you!" She pointed until she filled her quota of rebels.

"What about me?" a little boy asked and raised the stump of his arm into the air and shook it devoutly.

"And most of all, you!" Christina swung him up into her arms. "There's a mission for everyone! Now gather round, my comrades! We've much to do before the dawn."

Chapter 20

The guards raced in a column toward the noisy violence in Blockhouse No. 7.

"Louder! Louder! I can't hear you!" Christina wailed. She pulled the mattress from a cot and threw it to the floor, then clanked the metal frame against the wall. "More! More! More!"

Sondra smiled gleefully, ripped her mattress open, and tossed the stuffing into the air. "And this! And this! And this!" She caught Christina's eye. "Look at them!" she shouted. "Hell, pure hell!"

Christina looked about the room. Chaos, disorder, pent-up fury released one hundredfold, and eyes that shone with life and hope. It was a chance, a stab at freedom, and they had chosen to accept its price. "Courage begets liberty!" she shouted, prodding them, molding their fear with strength. She imagined the sun shining on their pale, sickly faces. Freedom would be sweet.

The door clanked opened with sudden violence, and the Nazis clattered in and down the aisles. They halted, pointed their guns, and Christina dared herself not to break. She scanned the fierce, concentrated eyes of the Nazis and then swiftly locked onto those of the children. Their eyes were steady and clear, their expressions unruffled.

They were ready, she thought. Now or never, and she stomped her foot, one, two, and before she stomped three, the platoon fell where they stood, their guns and helmets clattering wildly to the floor. She stomped again and a second regiment of children scrambled for their guns and held them at bay.

After another stomp, the third regiment of children under the cots released the Nazis' ankles and tied them up with strips of ticking. A cheer rang out.

"Well done, my comrades!" Christina shouted. "We have guns!"

She was functioning on sheer fright now. The most difficult part was yet to come, and she had lost control of the children. It was mass confusion; pushing and shoving to observe the row of sour German faces. Some of the children spat and cursed them, while others wailed in fright.

Christina yanked a riot whistle from a guard's neck and blew the unforgettable sound that announced sure death, and suddenly, voices stilled and expressions froze.

"It is time!" Christina screamed, her eyes large and brilliant. "Guns in the lead five abreast! Girls with babies form in the rear!"

Lines formed. Christina calculated the risks: babies who cry, the crippled, the sick, the fearful and hesitant who stay behind. She waved at the one-armed boy. "You! To the rear, with your handgun! Help the stragglers!"

There was no time to voice doubts, and Christina squelched the faintest desire. Freedom was an inch away, and no one wanted to believe he might die. With her gun pointed, she burst out of the door. Five abreast, they ran as fast as they could manage, the stragglers coaxed by the armless boy; the weak, sick, and crippled carried by the able-bodied.

Suddenly, Laurent's war strategy came to Christina, and she bolstered courage thinking about it: exploit to the maximum the vulnerability of the enemy. Position was everything, the tactical advantage. Refrain from wasting resources where resistance was stubborn. Wars were won by will and will was all they had.

The horde trammeled through darkness down the corridor. Dawn was on the horizon, and Christina knew that their cover would vanish soon. They had to make it out of the blockhouse, past the guards, and sustained by the forest and a climate they were used to, all she had to accomplish was the radio link with the Resistance. They neared the door, benumbed of consequences, all too horrible to contemplate.

"This is it!" Christina cried. "Aim those guns! Squeeze those triggers, my little soldiers!" A rain of artillery blanketed the door and it slammed to the ground. A guard lay dead and three others ran toward the mob and sprayed them with gunfire.

"Fire and run!" Christina charged ahead, her finger frozen on the trigger. Children dropped to the left and right of her. Backup ran around to the front line and took aim.

Muzzle flashes lit, and the guards dropped to their knees and doubled over.

"Help the wounded," Christina cried, "and run for the forest!"

The moon shone and lit a path on the snow toward a thicket of trees. With adrenaline soaring and spirit proliferating thrice-fold, they swiftly pummeled toward it.

"Hit the ground!" Christina shrieked.

Planes buzzed overhead and from their bellies streamed parachuted fighters spiraling downward like cottony seeds blown from catkin clusters. Their chutes gleamed against the moon as the clouds swallowed them. Christina sprang to her feet and waved the horde of ragamuffins forward.

Almost! Almost! The words screamed in her brain as she watched the line of trees grow near. She turned and eyed the snarl of arms and legs racing behind her, and their alert faces, and the resolution each wielded, driven to the wall.

They would make it; she could touch the trees if she reached out. The children ran in waves around her into the dark, safe forest, dodging here and there the fallen branches and small ravines, and they bawled with joy as they collapsed against one another.

The escape siren sounded, and Christina frantically scanned the compound, all two hundred acres, row upon row of concrete dormitories surrounded by barbed wire.

Suddenly, she eyed her destination: the sign read: 'Blockhouse No. 2', the largest of the buildings near the landing site of the parachute fighters.

Sondra looked at the object of Christina's concentration.

"You would be a fool!" She clasped Christina's shoulders and shook her almost violently. "You can't! In less than an hour, it will be daybreak. You will never make it through the barrage of fighters. There is nothing you can do for your sister now!" They watched another swell of parachutes float from the clouds.

"I'm going!" Christina snarled, and now it was sinking in, outrage upon outrage, she realized.

"Your sister is most likely dead!" Sondra stormed. "What about us? We wait here helplessly while you search for a ghost?"

Christina looked hard into Sondra's face, resentment burned, and suddenly she hated her as much as she hated the Nazis.

"How short your memory is! I am going to find my little sister, and I will probably die doing it, but it does not matter. She is my life, and at least for now, I have that, which is more than I can say for you! You would do well to take a stand for something! Take the children and disappear into the forest. There's a safe house outside La Gleize, about ten kilometers west of here."

Christina clipped a fresh magazine onto her weapon and then ran to a line of trees toward the blockhouse. Halfway there, she stopped and scanned the entrance. Searchlights swept, and she watched an echelon of soldiers stream from Blockhouse No. 2. She waited for the lights to sweep by, inhaled, and then bolted into the open. Almost there, she dropped to the ground and crawled on her belly, inch by inch, toward the north end of the building.

She watched the soldiers, armed and uneasy and tried to count them, but it was impossible. She crawled steadily, keeping the blockhouse in her sight. After a while, she stopped to rest. A searchlight beam crisscrossed the field, played along the edge of the forest, and then reflected back.

Suddenly, a long white shaft split the darkness and rested upon her body. She froze, every muscle locked, and peered ahead at the blockhouse, then left and right of her, and then scanned the forest. A rabbit scampered into its burrow and a fox waited stealthily nearby. The light swept again and the rabbit hopped out and blindly gaped into the glare.

She heard the fox panting as it circled for the kill. The searchlight swept toward the line of trees, and the forest came alive, singing and chirping a jubilant chorus. The fox pounced on its death leap and locked its jaws. The rabbit convulsed, and then the singing convulsed, mournful and repentant, then despaired into silence.

Christina's mind shouted, No! And repeated it over and over with her eyes shut tight so she did not have to see the slaughter, but something inside of her burst. Before the scream reached her lips, a guard rolled her over and shouted cruelly into her face.

"Lorelei!"

Christina knew well the German legend about the siren who led men to destruction, and she looked up at the Nazi's deranged grin and let out a strangled cry. He placed a heavy boot on her weapon and jerked her upright.

"*Schweinhund!*" Pig dog! he shouted and then drove his fist into her face.

Chapter 21

The hours before noon melted one into the other as Christina drifted in and out of consciousness. She fought to remain alert and face the monster who stood before her, but callously, the *gauleiter* continued his interrogation until she could take no more, and her head fell limply onto her chest.

An interpreter dropped into a chair beside her.

"It is of no use," he spoke in German to the *gauleiter*. "We will have to wait until she regains consciousness."

Her mind circled. The cry was small, buzzing, whirling, the intensity increasing with each revolution. A voice boomed from inside: You will endure! Nicolette will live in unrepentant horror if you do not! You are not lost; you will find your way. Do not lose heart; hold fast, and conquer your pain. You must! You must! You must!

The *gauleiter*'s anxiety was mounting minute by minute. "I would dispose of this American spy with my own hands if my Führer would permit, but I am nothing but a lowly petty tyrant, and he's relinquished her to Colonel Montrose, a cripple of a man, wheelchair bound and bandaged from head to toe. Imagine! My Führer expects results from a man half-dead!"

He stood with his shoulders back, his stomach sucked in and talked of the day when he would rise in rank above all of his superiors and bring them all fawning to his feet. "Inform me of the Colonel's arrival immediately!" he ordered the guards.

The name hung in Christina's mind, and she realized the terror unfolding before her.

Colonel Montrose would utilize torture beyond her comprehension. "Death will be slow and agonizing if you are caught," Rasha had explained.

She rolled her head toward her shirt pocket and eyed the pill. Rasha's clemency would deliver her to the chrysalis of Heaven, and gradually she gleaned solace in the contemplation. She thought of the inevitability: hoping against hope that she would find Nicolette, her mind incessantly plotting, never free of the faith that she would.

She thought back in time when father had placed Nicolette, fresh from God, into her hands, and how she had been the light of her life, but never so much as now, when death was near and despair was weakening her resolve and casting her into a listless stupor.

She lifted her head and eyed the legless figure wheeling in the door toward her, past the line of guards and the *gauleiter*. He stopped before her, wrapped his fingers around her hair, and pulled her into his stout, jowly face. An eye was missing, but the other scrutinized her maliciously, and she maneuvered a defiant smile.

"Jawohl!" he gloated in recognition. He recalled her voice from the radio. How could he forget that voice, he thought, the voice the Nazis had taken to battle, the

wounded, and the homesick. He looked at her torn face and remembered her beauty. He laughed.

"My Führer will be avenged."

Christina's mind flashed on grandfather's look of horror when she refused to sing for his Führer, and now retaliation would be more brutal than she could imagine.

Colonel Montrose slid his knife from his sheath and ran his finger along its edge, then flicked a drop of blood into her face. Something hard and steady rose from her belly, and she felt her fear slip away as she spat on him.

His eye froze on hers, stunned, and then he threw his knuckles into her face. The small cry began anew: buzzing, whirling, the intensity increasing with each revolution. She shook her head swiftly from side to side and then lifted her chin again.

"*Deutschlandlied!* Sing!" he shouted, nodding affirmatively with a horrible grin. He was jeering, baiting her with his cruel smile.

She knew all too well the 'Song of Germany'. *"Nein!"* she shouted and clenched her teeth to steady her jaw.

He beat her again, she did not falter but laughed freely with pleasure at his vexation.

"*Deutschlandlied!* Sing!" he demanded.

"Nein!" she cried, choking back the pain. I will not cry, she commanded herself. By God, I will not cry!

He beat her with a force that made her vault with screams, screams that came violent and continual. Then, at long last, there was no pain, as if God Almighty had exalted her to a berth of lasting bliss transcending all suffering. She slumped in exhaustion.

Where is your courage? The voice boomed again. You are a Cross, steady and hard as granite, like your father before you who fought with pride and strength for his beloved *Republik Österreich!*

"*Deutschlandlied!* Sing!" Colonel Montrose shouted, his expression absent of any trace of humanness.

Christina hung her head, her mind shouting the words that had always seen her through: Father! Father! Father! She wept inwardly. She could not stand it now. She could not will her mind to be silent. The memories assailed her, circling, swooping, tearing in and out of her brain; recollections that hurt and were futile: Father, Mother, Marcel, Nicolette, those who were dead and gone. Things that were peace and family and security, gone forever.

"*Deutschlandlied!* Sing!" Colonel Montrose's tone was unmistakable. Death was near. Her stubborn pride beckoned with urgency. She must look him in the eye, she commanded herself, and she struggled to lift and run them over him. She must! Another swell of pain. She drifted in and out, her eyelids twitching over what felt like broken glass.

Colonel Montrose shouted something, something registering finality, and the horror washed back over her. Never had she realized the power of thirst, and she wanted to swallow. Father! Father! She cried inwardly again. She prayed for redemption, and gripped by a newborn catharsis, somehow felt liberated from everything evil, harmful, and painful, as if her father were guiding her every thought and move.

Her eyes flicked up, and for a timeless moment, they locked onto the Colonel's. She was not small and frightened any longer. Defiantly, she cleared her throat and forced her broken jaw apart.

There was complete silence now. Dimly, through the haze, she became aware that the guards had circled her, and their eyes gazed hopefully in anticipation, as if her voice would carry them home. Blood streamed in gushes from her mouth as she opened it and struggled unavailingly for what seemed like hours until her voice finally came:

"God bless America, land that I love;
Stand beside her and guide her, through the night with a light from above,
From the mountains to the prairies to the oceans white with foam, God bless America, my home sweet home."

Colonel Montrose shook with rage. His bloated face exploded with purple splotches and saliva rolled from the corners of his mouth. He wiped it with his arm and then took aim with his knife. Christina hung her head, sweating with fear, and for the last time, she saw Nicolette, felt her warmth, and smelled her hair. The image comforted as if something safe circled her.

She watched her run through autumn leaves: playing, laughing, throwing heaps into the air, and letting them fall back onto her. She saw home, the old porch, and her father's rocking chair welcoming her through the shadows of the prickly ash. She breathed deeply and felt the quiet hush of the hilly countryside and the warmth of the sun coursing through her.

She thought of Liam and wondered if he were still alive. His kind ways and calm dignity, so much like father, and now she realized why she had loved him so. She summoned his words, and suddenly, she longed for the things he had spoken of: love's passion, pleasure, and all the tempestuous emotions of a young girl's feelings; things she had buried so deeply with Laurent.

Yes, Laurent had loved her as much as a man could love, her likeness always in his eyes, his heart in her hands. If only she could have let him in.

The *gauleiter* came forward, whispered something to Colonel Montrose, and then wheeled him toward the door. Without another thought, Christina slid her chin down and over her pocket until Rasha's pill appeared, and then pressed her tongue onto it.

**

News of the *kinderkamp* had spread rapidly through frontline units and had a staggering effect. American conviction stiffened, and Major Miller received full support from his general. Laurent had proposed a task of enormous size and complexity, requiring Major Miller to pull two divisions out of line, wheel them east, and launch an assault, all in three days. The R.A.F. had dropped explosives, Sten and Bren guns, grenades, and bazookas from parachutes.

By noon, the regiments were positioned in the frontline trenches five hundred yards from the *kinderkamp* and Blockhouse No. 2. Laurent mapped out a detailed plan for a daylight attack under enemy fire. The attacking Second Division units would be pulled back through their rear battalions, which would cover their withdrawal.

The movement would be repeated until the entire regiment was safely back under the cover of the forest.

Laurent and his unit would take up a position as soon as he was inside the building.

"Delouse that field!" Laurent shouted.

Major Miller signaled to his engineers and pointed toward a clearing. "Snow's too deep!" he hollered. "It'll weaken the signals from the mine detectors. We'll have to dig by hand. If the minefield is too dense, we'll explode the snakes."

"Lay the daisy chains, that'll stop the bastards in their tracks!" Laurent grinned at his good friend. "Combat units, wrap yourselves in your parachutes and crawl on your bellies to Blockhouse No. 2. Second Division, wait for my signal."

He dug into his pocket and handed Major Miller an envelope. "This is for Christina," he instructed. "She is at the *Maquis'* headquarters in Bastogne."

"Give it to her yourself!" Major Miller barked. "You've got my best storm battalions, and hard on their heels you've got me, and by damn, I'll overrun everything that stands in my path!"

Laurent grinned in agreement and put the envelope back into his pocket. "Advance and smash!" he shouted, then waved the lead column forward toward Blockhouse No. 2.

When they arrived, he established a solid line of defense blocking the northernmost entrance to the outer blockhouse. He looked hard into the sky and scanned it for fighter bombers. "No activity, we've crawled right under their noses! Blow the door before they organize their countermeasure!" He gave a signal, and the door exploded in a ribbon of gunfire.

The pill dissolved, revealing the bitter taste of the foxglove plant. Christina swished it under her tongue and held it there. Death would be effortless now, she thought. Effortless for the body, unbearable for the mind, it still wanted life: the taste, smell, and feel of it. Body and mind in constant opposition, one worn and battered, the other strong and sure—strong in body, strong in mind—rare to find such a quality.

Now she knew of her father's battle. She felt blood stream down her face and watched as it splashed onto her lap. She was grateful Laurent had not seen her strung up like this. She thought of his words, and they gave her comfort: "*Beaux yeux, mademoiselle.* You are so very beautiful. There is not a woman in France who could compare to you. You are what I want."

A cache of sensual fantasies returned: the beginning, his arm around her as they danced, and the excited feeling she had felt when his face touched hers. He was with her now, the man in the Foreign Legion, dressed in the white uniform with gold shoulder braids and tan, swarthy face with lapis blue eyes and square white teeth.

She had pushed him from her life without a single thought, and now he possessed her in a way she had never dreamed possible. It was as if he had taken her soul, her thoughts and desires, and swept her up gently into the wind.

She watched the *gauleiter* wheel Colonel Montrose in front of her. He screamed a fanatical scream. She hated him, hated with a force that overpowered her fear, and suddenly she thought of all the courageous French soldiers who lay rotting deep in the earth; for the first time, she felt akin to them; felt one in their terror, their hatred, and their convictions.

It would be an honor to lie beside them, she thought. She knew her father's horror: to be driven from a place so beautiful without so much as a look back, a dear homeland turned over to a bunch of marauding monsters. His blood was in her, allegiant blood, and she would die recklessly and hard for the things she believed in.

She swallowed hard, and the pill dissolved and coated the back of her throat. Soon, the lullaby came back, and her father's large, rough hands cradled her face, his sweet voice softly traversing over and through her.

**

Through the flail of gunfire and bursting bodies, he saw her chained like a dog to a cement wall. Her unmistakable ebony hair hung on her face, and her glistening eyes were unseeing. In spite of her hideous wounds, she was still beautiful to him. He ran to her, the sense of shock and dread choking him as he tried to call out her name.

Death unfolded, and there was only blackness, a vast nothingness that was peace. Soon, she followed a brilliant nebula into an obsidian womb, then back into the light of day. It wasn't an ending, only a beginning. Spring encompassed her, and she breathed the fresh-plowed fields. Meadowlarks warbled and flitted across the grasslands above the burr oaks where nuthatches harped from gnarled burrows.

She watched as the sun set its crimson beams over long prairie grasses, and after it passed, the clouds were ivory and amethyst in the eventide. She felt safe, wrapped in Laurent's arms as he gently rocked her, felt his sweet tears meet her face, and the rhythm of his breathing as he stroked her hair. Faintly, she heard him weep; "I have found her, Christina. Nicolette is safe, and she is waiting for you."

She felt herself smile. No, it was not over, she thought. It was not finished: the dreams, the good times. Her loved ones would trace her image in the tranquil summer clouds and know she watched over them, cloaked in the wind, its sound, and movement, her course drawn by the path of their love.

They would remember times past when things were good when the wind blew gentle waves across the clovers and wild indigos and the cattails and sedges that grew in the marsh near the river. Come eventide, they would sit in the rocking chair on the old porch and watch the moon glitter in the twilight and know she was there with them.

Christina looked at Laurent lovingly, then dropped her head from his arms and stopped struggling.

Laurent's face went hot with rage, and his eyes, which he could not pull from hers, stung with insufferable revenge. Mechanically, he rose to his feet and eyed the bloodbath surrounding him. It was near the door, the grotesque heap of flesh draped upon the wheelchair. He stormed toward it, grabbed the head, and pulled it back by its hair. The face looked at him and exulted an unmistakable gloat even in death; in his mind, he heard his triumphant laughter ring out.

He felt the hatred, hot and hard, rise in his throat and fill him up. He dispersed a long, petulant wail, like a bear shot in the heart, and let his tears overflow his eyelids and run unabashedly down his face. He hurled himself at the corpse and pummeled it with his fists; the more he beat, the more his fury grew, unabated, sweeping through him.

Jean-Baptiste ran frantically toward him and pulled him off. "The troops have liberated the blockhouses, sir," he shouted. "There's no more time. We must go!" Laurent sagged against Jean-Baptiste. "I cannot go," he said, looking at Christina's broken body hanging from the wall.

"You must, sir! The place will be crawling with krauts in a matter of minutes!"

Jean-Baptiste ran to Christina and aimed his gun at the chains that restrained her arms. He fired, and she tumbled forward onto him. He lifted her over his shoulder, then nodded toward the door. "Let's go, sir."

Jean-Baptiste placed Christina onto a blanket of beech leaves deep in the forest. The sun sent long golden columns of light sifting through the branches onto her face. Laurent kneeled down beside her and cleaned her wounds. He stared at her miserably, then lifted her to his breast and rocked her in his arms.

"Wake up, Christina," he pleaded. "Wake up, please wake up."

Her head lolled sideways, and the sight of it broke Jean-Baptiste. He held his head in his hands and began to weep, and suddenly, he was overcome with a compulsion to die himself, to be departed from a world of savage death and destruction, away from the bodies that had surrounded him all day. He felt an arm slip around his chest, and he tried to strangle the heave of grief.

"It is all right, my comrade," Laurent comforted. "It is good to weep. It seems we have forever lived on the brink of death, and now, somehow, I feel envious, and yet offended, that she has left me, gone to a peaceful place where I have never gone, far away to the edge of it all; I'll never know where until I die."

Jean-Baptiste caught his breath, took out a kerchief, and blew his nose. "Strange thing about peace," he said with a sigh. "It only exists in death."

"Perhaps your children will know peace." Laurent tried to imagine it looking at the death and ruin around him, and suddenly he thought of Nicolette. He wanted to squeeze his eyes shut and let the tears gush from them. He felt battered, as battered as the tricolor waving over the *Maquis* as they wallowed past him toward the command post.

He picked Christina up and began to follow them. He stopped for a moment and looked at the cruel, pallid countryside, then turned and plod back toward Jean-Baptiste.

"I have nowhere to go," he said. "I cannot bear to bring her to Nicolette." He sat down and held her tightly to his breast again, and they both watched her until the sun died and fused into the horizon.

After darkness fell, Laurent lifted Christina into his arms and began to walk.

"Where you headed?" Jean-Baptiste stirred and rubbed his eyes.

"Home."

Jean-Baptiste stood and fell in beside him, and they tramped toward the nearest line of trees. By sunrise, they saw the Amblève River and the road on the south bank. Stragglers from a dozen units joined them and trudged toward the American command post located in a schoolhouse in Trois-Ponts. An army jeep skewed haphazardly on the ice and slid to a stop next to them.

"Hop in, sir," he hollered to Laurent.

Laurent walked past and removed the blanket from Christina's face. The sun cracked through the clouds, and he pointed her toward it. "Do you think she can feel it?" he asked Jean-Baptiste.

Jean-Baptiste waved the GI on. "Where she's gone, sir, she'll feel everything good. No frostbite, no pain, no war, nothing bad. More than I can say for the rest of us bastards. Only good thing about this weather," he said gratefully, "it grounded the Nazis and paralyzed their bombers."

He stopped and shoved straw back down his boots and watched as Laurent sidestepped the winding column of soldiers, then walk to a bridge and onto a narrow road. The sign pointed toward the village of Saimes. Jean-Baptiste fell in line and let him go.

He could see the small, stone château tucked into the crescent of the wooded hill as if it were yesterday. A cluster of turrets and cupolas jutted from the roof, and a fragment of glass in the high-arched window glistened in the sun. Wild boar and deer wandered from the thickets and nibbled seedlings in the yard.

Soon, he reached the cobblestone path that led to the courtyard. It was a snow-capped tangle of woodland underbrush and ruin, except for the crosses that marked the graves of his mother and father. His shoulder nudged the door and it swung open easily. He lit a candle on the wall sconce, then walked down the hall and up the staircase and placed Christina on his bed. He turned from her and walked to the portal overlooking the terrace.

"Why?" he cried, looking out at the watermill frozen at the last turn of autumn. He pounded the wall with his fist. "Why, Why, Why?" A dozen times he had wanted to return to Bastogne and take her with him, but he knew it would be too dangerous, no place for a woman. And what did it matter now? She had gone anyway.

"Damn her!" he shouted. He looked at the forest, thick with spruce and chestnut, the countryside opening here and there to snow-capped vistas. It had been a long time since he'd taken comfort in a woman's body, and he had wanted her, wanted to bring her to his childhood home and marry her and raise a family. The sound of her voice filled his head, the sweet smell of her, the soft touch of her; things that had aroused him so readily, things that no longer existed.

He looked at the crosses in the courtyard, and the pressure in his throat choked, and he wondered if he could live without her. For the first time in his life, he had welcomed love and his reliance upon her love.

And now she was gone. He wanted to scream and curse his futility, but he had to think clearly. He thought of Nicolette, and he brightened for a moment. *It cannot end here*, he thought. He had promised Christina, and he would hold dearly to that promise. He gathered himself, the last of his strength, and turned toward Christina, bent over her and kissed her, and without looking back, walked out the door.

**

Nicolette clenched him with her small, bony fingers and buried her face on his shoulder, and sobbed. "They's all gone, every last one of them—they's all fairy angels in Heaven. I want to go, too."

Laurent looked ahead and began to tremble. He had little grasp of a child's thoughts until now. It was so simple, the solution so rudimentary through her eyes. He was sick of duty, of war, of living, and suddenly he wanted to go with her, to be with the fairy angels. His business was finished on earth. The city of Strasbourg was next to fall—a barter for American lives.

General Eisenhower had ordered a pullback rather than risk the entrapment of the U.S. Seventh Army. It was up to the *Maquis* to remove their forces from Allied control and defend Strasbourg on their own. The situation would be catastrophic for his compatriots, and for what? Yet another obscure headline for an American newspaper.

A nurse approached Nicolette and filled a needle from a vial, then poked it into her arm. Laurent gently placed her on the bed and watched her until she drifted to sleep. She was different now; war had taken its toll, and she would never be the same again. The twinkle in her blue eyes was gone, as was her will; the dread of another day, the constant murmur eating away. The feeling he had was like nothing he had ever known.

He, a man who had scorned weakness, now found himself helpless in its grip. He had mastered war, or so he thought: the killing, the calculations, the weapons, and the rest. The voices of his men sounded faint, calling for their mothers as they lay scattered in a field. He watched them, their expressions, the sounds of their screams and thrashing boots. The outside world had not an inkling of their horror: the burning flesh, hair, and bones. He could not live another day with what he knew.

A command jeep drove up the driveway, and the driver hopped out, saluted, and then opened the door. Laurent slid into the back seat with Nicolette in his arms.

"Saimes," he said.

"Yes, sir!" The young man snapped another salute. Fresh snow covered the road. It was lined with broken buildings; windows and doors were crossed with scrap wood, and all the side streets were barricaded. There were no soldiers, no vehicles moving. *It felt like Sunday*, Laurent thought, when he was a young boy. They passed a graveyard, and rows of debris jutted from the snow and marked the graves: a stovepipe, a walking cane, a crucifix made from table legs.

Soon, they left behind the burned-out city blocks, and the beauty and splendor of the countryside opened before them. The sun rose high and made a blinding dazzle on the ice-covered evergreens. It was as he remembered, this stretch of pastoral refuge, and the peace of it had stayed with him, helping to muffle the howitzers, the bombardments, and the din of war.

Nicolette looked up at him and smiled. Her sockets were dark holes. He knew her horror; she was a soldier, every inch a brave little soldier, and Christina would have been proud. He hugged her tightly. The scent of her hair was Christina's: her eyes, her skin, and her voice. He forced it back. He was breaking, and he could feel it, the suffocating whirl closing in on him.

The jeep pulled up to the courtyard. Laurent stepped out, waved the driver on, and carried Nicolette into the château. He parted the blankets and kissed her cheek. "We are home, *mon p'tit chou-chou*," he said softly. He propped her up on a *couchette* and tucked the blankets securely around her. "I'll light the stove and make some tea."

He walked to the kitchen, lit an oil lamp, then broke the wooden slats from a chair and placed them into the stove. He leaned from a broken window, chipped icicles from an eve, and put them into a kettle. He found two small silver cups in a cupboard. The room was rapidly warming, and he took off his coat and gloves, then brought Nicolette into the kitchen and sat her at the table.

"It was once a beautiful home." He smiled and placed a teabag into her cup and poured in hot water.

Nicolette's eyes scanned the room and then settled on a photograph of a young man dressed in a riding suit.

"Is that you?" she asked.

Laurent took the photograph from the wall, inspected it, and then placed it before her. He pulled from his canvas bag a bottle of cognac, uncorked it, and poured it into his cup.

"That was my grandfather. You would have liked him; he liked horses."

"Who killed him?"

"No one. He died of old age."

Nicolette shrugged, and suddenly, he understood. He leaned forward and stroked her curls. She smelled of wind and evergreen and adolescence. She was eight years old, but savagery had stunted her—a child doomed to the heart of aggression. He could not face it, nor understand it. Nothing beaconed the reason children should suffer war.

"My grandfather was a hero, a brave man," he said. "He fought in the Rhine Army and soon became marshal of France." His grandfather's words began to fill him: "Until the loss of the body, you will fight. Fight to assure justice for the glory of France and those who have already died for it."

Great were those times, he thought. There was justice and faith, and men believed as none do now. All is changed, another guise, and now with dead certainty, he knew his grandfather's words were futile.

"Can I see Christina?"

Fresh grief flooded. He threw another cognac down. His thoughts were unbraiding, one from the other. He rose to his feet, and Nicolette ran from him, up the stairs, her tattered blanket flying behind her. She opened the door, peered in, and ran to Christina's side. The wide-eyed glittery look she gave him as he peered into the room took his breath, and he kneeled and took her in his arms.

"She's cold," she cried. "Put a blanket on her. She looks like my friend Marie when she went to Heaven."

"She's asleep," Laurent choked. "Look at her, she's at peace, and she is thinking of you, watching you." Christina was lying on his childhood bed and wearing the antique wedding ring he had slid onto her finger.

Nicolette took Christina's hand and held it, and with two little fingers, she rubbed round and round the little gold wedding band. "I miss her, I miss her so much," she cried. "I want to go. I want to be with her and pa and my friend Marie."

A silence fell between them as they watched Christina lying on the featherbed. He was thinking recklessly now. No, he was not deranged. He had understood Nicolette's reasoning: too much pain, the thought of living and facing hopeless odds. Wasn't the prospect of being with Christina paramount? He could well picture the shock of his comrades. Was it wrong?

Nicolette climbed up and lay beside her. "I want to go," she pleaded. "You said everything in Heaven was beautiful and safe."

He took a long time to answer, and then finally, he spoke. "You have lost everyone, and so have I, and who knows how long this war will last. I have done everything in my power to help, but it seems only minuscule. I know my spirit has left, and I cannot go on."

"These people, the Germans, are unbeatable, capable of detail, discipline, knowledge, and determination beyond any civilization known to me. Reason and logic are lost, slaughter has become a delight, and it has unleashed a holocaust of war that will end in the destruction of the world. I torture my thoughts with the same questions over and over again. Am I mad?"

The discernment in Nicolette's expression calmed him. She knew of what he spoke, and there was no need to ramble on. He opened his pack and took out a vial of pills.

The words were scarcely breathed as he knelt beside her. "Take them," he said and put them to her lips. He watched her swallow, and soon she closed her eyes.

"Goodbye, my fairy angel," he whispered. His throat clamped shut and he struggled to finish his words, losing belief in what he had done. Soon, her tattooed arm fell limply from the bed. From her hand dropped the fossil. He picked it up and then slumped to his knees.

**

Jean-Baptiste entered the bedroom. After a few moments, he reappeared on the landing. Grief filled him as he faced the sergeant. "They're dead," he said, "the three of them frozen solid." And his thoughts centered on something Laurent said the day Christina died: "Together they can long endure," he had whispered lovingly, "yet once they are separated, the hazel dies almost at once, and the honeysuckle soon after, and my sweetheart, it is so with us."

It was odd, but in some strange way, he was thankful Laurent hadn't lived to see the memo inked by the Allies retracting the order to abandon Strasbourg. Laurent had already won his battle, and at long last he was home, delivered to a peaceful place where he had never been, far away, and surrounded by the ones he loved.

For the first time in months, Jean-Baptiste felt himself at peace. He turned and traipsed back into the bedroom and spotted the amber rock on the floor.

He picked it up and held it to the light. He would prepare himself for battle again, he thought, while studying the enigmatic rock. Confident that with Allied help, the *Maquis* would prevent the Germans from linking up their forces. Strasbourg would be saved, and Hitler's aim of diverting American troops from the Ardennes would fail.

He rubbed the amber with his fingers, and then he looked away at the blue sky and snow-capped mountains.

In the distance, he saw the ivory-colored barrage balloons floating downward. It had already begun.